Bedford Square 1

Bedford Square 2

New Writing from the
Royal Holloway Creative Writing Programme

Foreword by **ANDREW MOTION**

JOHN MURRAY

© Polly Atkin, Clementine Bartholomew, Mary Couzens, Edward L. Fox, Philippa Gough, Nicholas Hollin, Michael Hughes, Janet Irving, J. A. Lake, Joanne Leonard, Maria Margaronis, Paul Maunder, Katherine Miller, Jade Milton, Jak Peake, S. G. Perry, Gillian Petrie, Sam Riviere, Louisa Scott, A. E. Watterson, Ellie Watts Russell, Hilary Whittam, Anna Whitwham 2007

Foreword © Andrew Motion 2007

First published in Great Britain in 2007 by John Murray (Publishers)
A division of Hodder Headline

The right of Polly Atkin, Clementine Bartholomew, Mary Couzens, Edward L. Fox, Philippa Gough, Nicholas Hollin, Michael Hughes, Janet Irving, J. A. Lake, Joanne Leonard, Maria Margaronis, Paul Maunder, Katherine Miller, Jade Milton, Jak Peake, S. G. Perry, Gillian Petrie, Sam Riviere, Louisa Scott, A. E. Watterson, Ellie Watts Russell, Hilary Whittam and Anna Whitwham to be identified as the Authors of the Work has been asserted by them in accordance with the Copyright, Designs and Patents Act 1988.

1

All rights reserved. Apart from any use permitted under UK copyright law no part of this publication may be reproduced, stored in a retrieval system, or transmitted, in any form or by any means without the prior written permission of the publisher, nor be otherwise circulated in any form of binding or cover other than that in which it is published and without a similar condition being imposed on the subsequent purchaser.

All characters in this publication are fictitious and any resemblance to real persons, living or dead, is purely coincidental.

A CIP catalogue record for this title is available from the British Library

ISBN 978-0-7195-6823-7

Typeset by Servis Filmsetting Limited, Manchester

Printed and bound by Clays Ltd, St Ives plc

Hodder Headline policy is to use papers that are natural, renewable and recyclable products and made from wood grown in sustainable forests. The logging and manufacturing processes are expected to conform to the environmental regulations of the country of origin.

John Murray (Publishers)
338 Euston Road
London NW1 3BH

Contents

Foreword by Andrew Motion 7

Mary Couzens • **Front Men** 11

Edward L. Fox • **Cobra Spirit** 23

Philippa Gough • **Herbert and Edi** 35

Nicholas Hollin • **Blog** 47

Michael Hughes • **Towards Dawn** 59

J. A. Lake • **Associations** 71

Joanne Leonard • **Come Home** 85

Maria Margaronis • **The New Order** 97

Paul Maunder • **The War on Error** 109

Jade Milton • **No Man's Land** 121

Jak Peake • **Rafael's Garden** 131

S. G. Perry • **Seraph** 143

Louisa Scott • **Marcy Meets Velda** 155

A. E. Watterson • **We are Bound for the Promised Land** 167

Contents

Ellie Watts Russell • **The Lodge** 177

H. C. Whittam • **Angerona** 189

Anna Whitwham • **Red Brick Estate** 201

Polly Atkin • **Ten poems** 213

Cleo Bartholomew • **Seven poems** 225

Janet Irving • **Seven poems** 237

Kate Miller • **Five poems** 253

Gillian Petrie • **Nine poems** 263

Sam Riviere • **Ten poems** 277

Foreword

The Creative Writing MA programme at Royal Holloway College started life in the autumn of 2004: there was one fiction group and one poetry group, and at the end of the course examples of their work were gathered in the anthology *Bedford Square*. This second collection, from the second year of the course, reflects two significant changes in its structure. Two more people are now involved in the teaching – the novelist Susanna Jones and the poet Jo Shapcott – and we have two fiction groups, not one.

Soon after the end of the first year, two of the prose-writers were given contracts for their first novels (Tahmima Anam – with John Murray – and Joe Treasure – with Picador) and one of the poets (Adam O'Riordan) received a major Arts Council writing bursary. Like everyone else involved in the course, I am delighted by these early successes, and also like everyone else I believe that rapid publication is not the only way to measure the value of the MA. The year spent on the course offers a unique opportunity for concentration, discovery and experimentation – for taking risks as well as finding ways to confirm and develop what already exists – and the rewards of that opportunity are clearly on show in this second anthology in the series.

The book is brimming with new energy and proper variety: it contains poems which play with a range of forms, voices and points of view, and short stories and novel-extracts which range widely through different times, geographies and states of mind. Some of the work shows the excitement of recent self-discovery, and some has a more settled confidence. But whatever its tempo and temper, it shares a common purpose: to be true to its original vision, and to combine technical skill with imaginative reach. In this sense,

Foreword

and like all the best anthologies of its kind, *Bedford Square 2* is an exciting celebration of the present, and a heartening glimpse of the future. It is as surprising, challenging, rewarding and intriguing to read the book as it has been for us all to work on the course together.

ANDREW MOTION

Mary Couzens

Mary Couzens hails from Philadelphia, Pennsylvania, and has lived in London for ten years.

Her creative writing began at the turn of the century, with a beginner's course at Morley College. By 2002, she had completed a Certificate in Creative Writing at Birkbeck College, University of London, and begun studies on a BA in Creative Writing and English at the University of Greenwich. That year, she was also diagnosed as dyslexic. However, after graduating with first class honours, she won a scholarship for the MA in Creative Writing at Royal Holloway.

Mary is currently working on her first novel, *Toast of New York*, inspired by her adventures on the New Wave music scene in the late seventies and early eighties, and completing an anthology of short stories, set in the sixties, entitled *Philadelphia Stories*. She is also editor and reviewer for the independent, ever-evolving online theatrical forum *EXTRA! EXTRA!*

'Front Men' is from the fourth chapter of her novel-in-progress *Toast of New York*.

Front Men

Sal said we should treat ourselves to a couple new albums for the auspicious occasion of his new front man's first visit to our dinky little apartment. So we got on the El and went downtown to Sam Goody's. The store was huge, and we didn't have a clue what we were looking for, so we headed for the 'new releases' section.

His bar buddies swore anybody who knew anything had been listening to a band called The Cars since their album came out last year. There was a separate display for that, so we figured it must be good. And his friend Johnny told him he should pick up an album called *Parallel Lines*, which we found a couple of copies of under 'B' for Blondie. The cover had a trashy-looking blonde on it, wearing a white dress that looked like a slip, standing in front of her male band with her hands on her hips. She reminded me of the figurehead on a ship. Apparently Johnny had been foaming at the mouth over her non-stop, ever since he'd seen her picture. But he didn't have the album in his collection; I had a feeling Mona might not like it if he did.

When I had more dough, I'd head back to Sam Goody's on my own. They had tons of albums by loads of bands I'd never even heard of like the B52s, who had beehives higher than the ones Aretha used to wear. Then, there was Elvis Costello, the English crooner, as my friend Frances called him. She fantasised about him something fierce during our lunch hour. Though I have to admit, I couldn't understand why. He seemed more like a bookworm than a heartthrob. At least The Cars had a couple of cuties in their lineup, especially that blond guy – Benjamin Orr. Only blonds weren't my thing. Which was probably one reason why I ended up with a guy with lots of dark, wavy hair, like Sal. Meanwhile, my spouse was spouting off about the kind of girl he liked.

That Debbie Harry's pretty hot stuff, he said, forking over my hard-earned cash. All the guys are talking about her. Guys would. There used to be a name for girls all the guys talked about. I didn't want to get him started on a rant, so I kept my mouth shut.

How do you know? I asked, glancing at a poster of Blondie on the wall.

They play her songs in the bar, he said. That's where me and Johnny first heard them. It never occurred to me that in a dumpy neighbourhood bar like that they'd play anything other than World War II's greatest hits.

Like most guys, Sal thought of rock bands as being mostly a guys' game, apart from that blonde chick in Fleetwood Mac, of course, and those bimbos in Abba that every boy I knew fantasised about since he was in diapers.

I imagined there was equal footing in the black music world, with who did what depending more on talent than looks, or how much skin was showing, than there was in rock. Then again, I heard the Supremes had a hundred wigs each in their heyday.

Sal always acted like he was an expert on everything, so I didn't elaborate on what I was thinking. But I was starting to realise he was a little out of it. For one thing, he still looked more like a guy from South Philly than a citizen of the world. And apart from that striped shirt he'd worn for his audition, I didn't see him making any effort to change with the times.

Whereas I was branching out, meeting all kinds of people in my new job. For example, Frances, who was helping me learn the ropes in the bank, was a veritable warehouse of information about bands, especially if they were from New Jersey and featured muscular single guys – for example, Bruce Springsteen. Yuk! She still had a picture of her old flame in her locker, but I could tell Mr Costello'd soon evict him. She'd first seen him, in all his geeky glory, on *Saturday Night Live*. He'd actually stopped singing one song, because he wanted to sing a different one – one that his record company warned him not to. I thought that was pretty cool of him. She said the words to his songs were great too. So Elvis the second went on my mental list of people to look out for, along with that band whose strange song kept playing in my head after hearing it on the fateful night I put my hair on the chopping block – Joy

Division. They only had one album and it wasn't easy to find. No wonder they called it *Unknown Pleasures*.

I was biding my time with the list I was building – the way you do when you look both ways before you cross the street. When I felt ready, I'd explore some of the things on my list. But for now, I was still getting it together.

I was daydreaming a lot more these days too. Sometimes, about a mysterious guy coming along, and appreciating me more than anybody ever had before – one who would never, ever think of cheating on me. Not that I could prove Sal was a cheater. At this point, he was only a *Cheetah*, because Malcolm, the 'man of the world' front man I was going to meet today, had picked him, Sal Salvato, from countless other guys, to be his guitarist, and the band was going to be called *The Cheetahs*. I'd heard so much about this guy Malcolm that I couldn't help but wonder what he was like. I wasn't going to have to wait long to find out. Sal told him to come over to our place at four and it was already one thirty.

What're you gonna make for dinner tonight? Sal asked, as we got up to the liquor store. That reminds me, we gotta buy beer.

We? You mean me.

Whatever, he said, pushing the glass door open, I'll pay you back when the band makes it. That line was becoming his new mantra.

Apart from a few beers here and there, booze per se was still uncharted territory to me. I'd had a one-night stand with vodka and gin when I was in high school. But, after one cocktail, I decided to give up drinking for ever. Mind you, that cocktail was in a sixteen-ounce glass, and tasted like fruit cocktail, instead of whatever was in it, so I had no trouble downing it on a dare. But in the wee hours of the morning, when an over-zealous cop spotted me, sitting by myself at a bus stop stone drunk, after my shit-scared friends had deserted me, I got picked up for curfew, and spent the night in jail. That's what I get for trying to drown out Fleetwood Mac.

If they'd have played James Brown records that night, we would have been dancing, instead of hanging around guys who were just making do, while they were drooling over their album covers. After I spent that entire summer living in fear that my parents would find out I spent a night in the slammer, I swore off booze for life. In future, I intended to stay as clean as David Cassidy looked.

And I actually managed to stay that way till I met Mona, a couple of years later. She loved beer with a passion. We'd inevitably get bored, sitting around on a Saturday night in front of her TV, so we'd usually wind up having a few brews. But we were nothing like Sal and Johnny, who were in serious danger of sprouting barstool barnacles. However, at the moment, I needed to find just the right liquid refreshment for our visiting VIP.

What kind of beer should we get? Sal asked, running his hand over the cases.

I don't know, I said, I'll leave that to you. The bell on the door jangled, indicating a new customer had come in. He was the spitting image of Sid Vicious. His dyed black hair seemed more like the matted fur of a dead animal. He stared at me and smiled, showing yellowed teeth. I inched a little closer to Sal to whisper in his ear.

It might be a good idea to buy some foreign beer, I said. He pulled back in surprise.

You know, that might just be a cool idea. After all, Malcolm's been around. Good thinking, Batgirl.

He'd been calling everything 'cool' ever since he met his future front man the day before. It got on his nerves when I used that word. I usually hated it when he called me Batgirl too. But right now I didn't care. When he strutted up the steps to the next level of the shop, I followed. I didn't dare look behind me. When we stopped in front of the stacks of imported beer, I finally took a glance downstairs. I needn't have worried. Sid now had two girls with him, one on each arm. They must have been waiting for him in the store. He'd need them to keep warm – his jacket was ripped to shreds. He kissed one of them on the mouth then turned to the other.

Wow, that guy's really going to town, Sal said, following my glance. That'll be me once this band gets goin'. He nudged me in the ribs, and chuckled, but I moved away from him, and ducked behind one of the stacks. Hey, what gives? he asked. You know you'll always be my number one fan.

I could have killed him. The guy must have heard Sal's remark too. As he was leaving, he turned and gave him the finger, clinging to his tramps as shields.

That bastard, I'll kick the shit out of him, Sal said. I grabbed hold of his sleeve, but I needn't have bothered. He wasn't exactly knocking himself out to go after the guy. Lots of things were smoke and mirrors with Sal. That was one of the things that worried me about him.

That little punk was into you, he told me, when we went up to the counter. It's that shittin' haircut of yours.

I thought of a lot of things I could say to that. But I kept them in my head, which is where I was hanging out most of the time I was with Sal these days. I couldn't wait till this band thing got started. At least it would give us something new to focus on. I wasn't sure I liked the kind of guys my new look was attracting either. But my hair was a conversation piece, and God knows I needed one of them to get me going sometimes. It also made me look different than most girls, which I didn't realise I preferred until after the fact.

Sal pointed to a black and white picture on the wall near the Budweiser – 'The Ramones' it said at the bottom.

Look at these guys – they all have the same last name. They must be related, he said.

They looked it. They all had long dark hair, with bangs that almost covered their eyes, especially the tall, skinny front man, with the shades. And they were all wearing the same clothes: jeans with the knees out, like they'd fallen down in them, with black leather jackets and black Converse sneakers. I never even knew Converse sneakers came in black. My brother had white ones when he played basketball in high school. They weren't exactly the coolest things you could wear.

When we got home, Sal went into a frenzy running in three directions at once. I just went out in the kitchen, loosened the lid on the salsa, and poured some tortilla chips into my chip n' dip dish. We'd bought Mexican beer. My boss, Mr Sanchez, said Dos Equus was the best. It was a lot more expensive than Rolling Rock, but for some reason I felt like I wanted to make a good impression too. It seemed more open-minded to drink beer from another country. And there was always the chance that it might help cover up the fact that Sal didn't know a thing about any of the music Malcolm raved about at the audition. While we were out, he'd mentioned a couple of bands his front man loved – The Stooges for one. But we couldn't find any of their albums in Sam Goody's, and as usual, he was too proud to ask.

While we were getting everything ready, Sal put The Cars album on. The first song, 'Just What I Needed', was catchy, and you could understand most of the words. You could sing along to this stuff, or even dance to it if you felt like it, cause the beat was pretty good too. I hadn't danced since I married Sal, apart from on special occasions, with Mona, in her living room. He didn't know how to dance.

I brought out four little cinnamon candles I'd stashed in the kitchen cupboard for next Christmas, and scattered them around the kitchen. We'd had a tree last year, but we didn't do much else when it came to decorating, apart from slapping a cardboard Santa Claus on the kitchen door, because a) I couldn't afford it, and b) I didn't have time to get anything else, since I only had one day off, and that was the holiday itself. I was working at Wanamaker's then, so I had to be in at eight o'clock the next morning for the big after-Christmas sale. When they opened the doors, it was like a stampede at the spastic corral. All I could see from where I was standing were middle-aged women pushing past each other, waving their free shopping bags in the air. Fortunately, most of them ran right past our department, because they already had enough underwear. These candles had seemed like an investment for next year when I bought them in Rite Aide after Christmas. But there was no time like the present.

While we were out, Sal had insisted on buying a heavy black Buddha-shaped incense burner in Woolworths, and he'd plunked it down in the centre of the mantel as soon as we came in. To me, it looked more like a bouncer than a Buddha. Patchouli incense is my favourite, but he said it reminded him of hippies, so we ended up getting musk instead. Our visiting man of the world should feel right at home now that the living room smelled like a brothel. Some of Wanamaker's most loyal customers were hookers – and they always wore musk perfume.

While Sal was spinning his wheels, I went into the bathroom to try my new black mascara. I'd never worn mascara before, and my hand shook a little as I tore the silver tube off its cardboard backing. I swept the tiny brush across my lashes like they said in the directions, and looked at my eyes afterwards. Wow! I was going to look better today than I ever had. That would serve Sal right. I took out my lipstick brush, outlined my lips in deep red, then filled them in with a rusty colour. I blotted my lips before I came out of the bathroom, but Sal still latched onto my arm like a truant officer, when I passed him in the hall.

What's with the paint? I told Malcolm you were a natural-looking girl – a homebody, he said.

Why? I asked, jerking my arm free, I'm always out – working. Ordinarily, he would have given his war whoop then, but for now, he had better things to do.

Holy shit, is that the time? he asked, pushing past me, slamming the bathroom door behind him.

I went into the bedroom and opened my closet door. I'd been living in my baggy black trousers all week, and they needed washing. I fingered the pair of black stretch jeans I'd picked up in last week's thrift shop hunt. They were a good fit. I decided to wear the long-sleeved, silky T-shirt with the oil paintings on it with them – dark green was one of my favourite colours. I'd just begun to wax my hair up when the doorbell rang. I froze.

Can you get that? Sal shouted through the bathroom door. I'm still shaving. Leave it to him to get five o'clock shadow at three forty-five. Shit! I'd have to step on the gas.

I grabbed a glop of wax and rubbed my hands together, pulling my hair out in all different directions, not just on top – that was better. The bell rang again.

Jesus Christ, what're you – afraid of your own shadow? Sal bellowed loudly. But I was way ahead of him. I opened the bedroom window and looked down at the blond head of the guy ringing the bell.

Be there in a minute, I shouted, slamming it shut before he had a chance to look up. Stepping into the jet-black sneakers I'd picked up as part of my winter collection, I went down the stairs at a trot. When I got to the bottom, I could see a guy's shape behind the blinds. He looked tall and slim. I threw the door open.

Hi, I said, before I could catch my breath.

Hi, the guy said, narrowing his eyes at me, as if I was standing in the sun. Then, a thin smile turned up the corners of his lips. He was dressed completely in black leather. The only guys I'd seen like that before were Hell's Angels. I backed up. He stepped inside. I leaned over him awkwardly to shut the door. My hair went against him, and I could feel his leather brush against the silk of my top.

You must be Sook, he said, taking my hand. I nodded. But I can't believe *you're* Sook.

An attack of my usual shyness was setting in. He held onto my hand for a moment, and I had the distinct impression that he was going to kiss me. He never actually moved towards me, but I felt as though he already had.

Come in, I said to him, in a voice like Minnie Mouse's. Which was a stupid thing to say – he was already in. He chuckled, let go of my hand, and gestured to the stairs.

Ladies first, he said. That was the oldest trick in the book. I didn't want some man of the world grabbing my ass on the stairs.

You first, I said, matter-of-factly. I need to bolt the door.

To keep the wolves out . . . he murmured, taking the stairs at a gallop. In a minute him and Sal were hugging each other at the top.

Paisan, Malcolm joked, keeping hold of his guitarist with one hand, and patting him on the back with the other. Once they'd gone through their ritual, they both turned to me.

You can come up now Sook, I don't bite, Malcolm said with a grin, baring his teeth.

As they went down the hall, toward the living room, I climbed the stairs, and went into the kitchen, wondering why my head was spinning. I thought Sal was a charmer, but he was small potatoes compared to this guy. Whew! I looked in the mirror on the cupboard door. My face was flushed and my eyes were throwing off sparks! I guessed Sal wasn't kidding when he said Malcolm had what it takes to be a super front man. I wondered what his songs were like.

Just as I was getting myself together, our guest strode out into the kitchen. When he looked at me, his eyes lit up like a Christmas tree, so I figured that was my cue to shove something cool into his hands.

Dos Equus? I asked, like the good little hostess. He looked impressed. I even have lime, I said, offering him a slice from the dish. That was a mistake. It gave him an excuse to come closer. After a minute's silence, side two of The Cars started playing in the living room. Malcolm was standing right in front of me, which made me glad I wasn't wearing a low-cut blouse, not that I'd have much to put into it. There'd probably be an explosion if he ever met my friend Mona and her party-doll boobs.

You are one quality chick, Malcolm said, taking the beer I offered, putting his other hand up to his chin, while he looked me over.

He didn't back up when Sal walked into the kitchen. He didn't have to. He was the front man.

Edward L. Fox

Edward L. Fox was born in New York in 1958 and lives in London. He is the author of *Obscure Kingdoms: Journeys to Distant Royal Courts* (1994), *Palestine Twilight: The Murder of Dr Albert Glock and the Archaeology of the Holy Land* (2001) and *The Hungarian who Walked to Heaven: Alexander Csoma de Koros, 1784–1842* (2001). This excerpt is from chapter one of his debut novel *Cobra Spirit*.

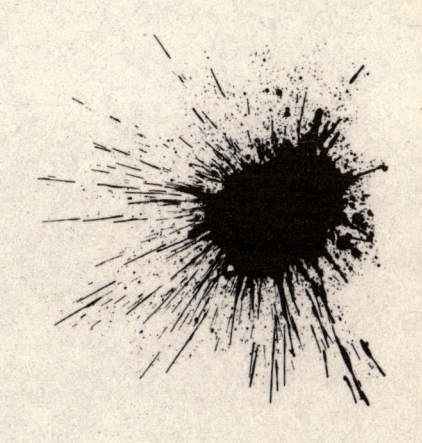

Cobra Spirit

I

A thief ran down to the waterfront, stumbled as he turned through the gate to the ferry landing, righted himself, and sprinted along the quay, clutching a tourist's bag in one hand. He shook sweat from his face; sweat poured down his naked back. He covered about a hundred metres before disappearing into a warehouse stacked with mahogany logs. Fireworks were exploding in the streets nearby, as if giving the thief covering fire. The day was the feast of Our Lady of Nazaré, and the Brazilian town of Belém, a place of ancient mildewy splendour at the mouth of the Amazon River, teemed with half a million worshipful revellers, each hoping for a blessing from the Virgin: a respite from illness, a job, a child, a miracle.

One person at least had been blessed that day. As he caught his breath in his dark hiding place, the thief found more than five hundred American dollars in the black nylon bag, as well as a passport and an air ticket. He made the sign of the Cross and muttered a prayer, then exhaled deeply but very quietly; he pocketed the money, returned the documents to the bag, and dropped it onto the cement floor. The thief sat very still in the dark, listening for the tread of a security guard, waiting for the moment he could emerge and return to the confusion of the festival.

Up on the deck of the MV *Narwhal*, two young people, a man and a woman, watched the thief as he ran for sanctuary. They were seamen, although only one of them had any experience of the sea. The woman was small and delicate and neat, and wore a white shirt and white jeans; the man was tall and long haired and wore a scruffy blue boiler suit. His hair was tied into a pony tail with an elastic band. From their vantage point on the deck, they kept vigil over the festival. Their job was to make sure that none of the fireworks that the revellers were throwing around – even though it was brilliant daylight – landed on the deck and set fire to anything.

It was their first time in Brazil, and everything they saw amazed them.

From its place of mooring, the ship commanded a view of the Avenida Presidente Vargas, a broad avenue that led down to the waterfront from the Basílica de Nossa Senhora de Nazaré, which stood at the town's highest point. The image of the Virgin, a wooden statue in a glass-fronted cabinet, surrounded by yellow and white plastic flowers, showered with rays of light by the Holy Spirit in the form of a dove hovering over her head, was being wheeled through the streets from its home in the Basílica on a wooden chariot, and people were crushing through the crowd to put their hands on the ropes with which it was slowly pulled down to the main square.

'Someone has just lost their identity,' said the man in the boiler suit, watching the thief emerge from his hiding place without the bag.

The woman replied, 'I wonder if anyone will come after him.' No one did; no one would. The thief was safe.

The fireworks died down, so it was safe to leave their post.

'Let's go inside,' the woman said, 'and hear what Seb has to say.'

'His Catholic Majesty.'

'His Serene Highness.'

'I'm not sure how serene he is at the moment.'

'We'll just have to take our chances.'

They walked down the bow deck and through an open door into the ship's interior glow where Seb was waiting.

This close to the Equator, the sun sets with heartbreaking speed. It grows swollen and huge, turns a brilliant orange, then crimson, and for a moment the world is immersed in a perfect twilight that is all the more sublime for being so fleeting. Just as one begins to inhabit this perfect world of colour, it disappears. Within a few minutes, total darkness has taken over.

With nightfall the festival metamorphosed into a vast outdoor party. Thousands jammed the boulevards of Belém to dance to pounding sound systems. Towering loudspeakers blared carimbó rhythm; cooks sold *pato no tucupi* – duck stewed in manioc juice – from smoking pans on rickety tables on the sidewalks. Vendors sold amulets and strange traditional remedies: crocodile teeth, bottled snakes, bunches of herbs. At the margins of this spiritual carnival the pious and the elderly walked the cracked streets in little processions of half a dozen, holding long beeswax candles, and offering for sale lengths of ribbon in honour of the Virgin of Nazaré. You tied one of these to your wrist, then prayed every day to the Virgin for what you wanted. When the ribbon wore and broke, the Virgin would grant you your wish.

Somewhere in this multitude of revellers, one atom of the crowd was moving differently from all the others. A young white man was elbowing his way through the mass of people as if he were trying to get somewhere in a hurry. He emitted the only signal of urgency in the entire time zone, yet the signal went undetected. No one he jostled against acknowledged his haste or even noticed him. He was barely a smudge of white in the corner of an eye as he rushed past. Certainly, no one made it easy for him to get through. He feared he was in danger, that he was being followed, that he might be lost, and that he might fail to get to where he was going in time.

He was moving away from the centre of the town, down the Avenida Presidente Vargas, on the same route that the statue of the Virgin had taken earlier, in the direction of the ferry landing. As he approached the waterfront the crowd thinned out, and the young man saw the river for the first time. He was sweaty and frightened and carried no luggage, and he had a two-inch long gash by his right ear, to which he pressed a handkerchief. He passed through the open gate to the ferry landing, and saw what he was looking for. It was not what he was expecting at all.

Arriving at a destination for the first time in darkness is disorienting, but the young man was so astonished by the appearance of the ship that he almost turned back. He then remembered he had nowhere to turn back to. It was a sleek modern craft, brand new and gleaming white, like a huge toy that had just been taken out of its box. It was moored beside an elderly Amazonian river boat that looked like a floating slum, listing alarmingly to starboard, with washing hanging from the railings, and paint peeling from the hull. Maybe this was the ship he was meant to be boarding; but no, there was the ship's name, MV *Narwhal*, spelt out in stylized uncial lettering at the bow, with a design of a narwhal underneath, with a tusk like a corkscrew, painted in the flowing primitive style of an ancient Celtic manuscript. This was the ship he was looking for.

It looked more like a yacht, a pleasure boat, than a working vessel. Even in the darkness, it seemed to glow: it was painted a glossy white of unreal pristineness: like something out of a magazine. The windows of the bridge sloped back like the windshield of a sports car, tinted an inscrutable mirrored grey. Above this an array of navigational and communications devices blinked and rotated and probed the skies.

Now he was no longer in a hurry. He walked very slowly towards the ship, studying it warily. The gangway was down, so there would be no difficulty boarding, if that was what he resolved to do. The lights were blazing inside, and he could see people moving at the windows. He stood still in the hot, humid, starless night, with the river lapping against the dock before him, his wound stinging with blood and sweat, and distant music pounding behind him, and felt relieved that no one had noticed him, that he could remain where he was, camouflaged in darkness, for as long as he needed to.

A chill shook his narrow shoulders. He was tired and thirsty, and he needed a bandage. On a ship like that, he realized, he could probably even have a shower, whatever else happened. Once he had put his hand on the railing he knew he had committed himself, and walked up the creaking metal gangway. For the moment, at least, he was safe.

2

The young woman arrived at John F. Kennedy airport, New York, on an overnight flight from São Paolo, sometime after seven o'clock in the morning. She was small, about five foot one, and she carried a heavy shoulder bag that was so big it made her list sideways. Walking through the airport in thin white sneakers, she could feel her ankles wobble and hurt. She separated from the crowd of mostly Brazilian passengers at the sign for the luggage carousels, not needing to stop there: she had rushed onto the plane without time to check in her bag. Sleep-deprived and nerve-racked, she drifted through the queues and corridors and the formalities of landing. Everything seemed muffled, to be not really happening.

At passport control she handed the official her plane ticket by mistake, then dropped her passport onto the floor. Squatting down to pick it up, she nearly fainted. The passport officer gave her a suspicious glance, then handed back the passport. With fumbling fingers she stuffed the documents into her bag, zipped it shut and headed for the exit.

Opaque glass doors slid open, and a crowd of faces appeared before her. Now she was in New York. The faces stared into hers, seeking a face they recognized. Taxi drivers and corporate limousine drivers held up signs with names on them, fishing for a person they didn't know, but none of the names were hers. (I could start a new life, she thought. I could just go up to one of these guys and say, Here I am. Let's go. It wouldn't be a bad idea.)

Outside, the damp, steely cold of a New York winter morning blew into her. She had been expecting this, but in the haste and confusion of her departure she had been unable to prepare for it. She wore scuffed white jeans and a man's blue denim jacket that was too big for her, borrowed at the last minute. It kept her warm enough on the journey up to now, but now she began to shiver. Everyone around her wore big puffy coats, scarves and hats. She found a luggage cart, yanked it from its queue, and dumped her bag onto it. Relieved of its weight, she looked around for a place to buy coffee. At least it would keep her hands warm. She found a Starbucks stand and bought some coffee. There was a time, not so long ago, when this would have been against my principles, she thought.

Outside, on the sidewalk, an icy rain was falling hard. The drops bounced off the tarmac. She stood in line for a taxi, coping with the cold. When the taxi came, she hefted her bag onto the back seat, then shuffled in beside it, forgetting to return the luggage cart to its base and retrieve her coins. She gave the driver an address in downtown Manhattan.

The driver's name (according to the framed licence on the partition that separated them) was Hajjaj Bin Yusuf. She hoped he understood English.

'Can you turn up the heating, please?' she asked. He waved his left hand and said something she couldn't hear, so she gave up, wrapping her hands around the warm paper cup. The taxi sizzled along the Van Wyck Expressway to the rhythm of its windshield wipers. She closed her eyes and wished she could sleep, just for a moment, but the dinning of the thoughts and voices that had kept her awake on the plane persisted without respite, circular, merciless: the unrelenting torment of a fresh grief, the endless rehearsal of what she would say when she got to her destination.

She was the bearer of bad news. Her name was Donna Winder, and she was on her way to meet a man she had never met. His name was Bob Schofield. He was the chairman of the Narwhal Foundation, and the owner of the MV *Narwhal*.

The taxi braked hard, jolting her forward, and stopped outside a brownstone in a tidy street of grand houses. She paid the driver, got out, squeezed between parked cars and walked up the steps to the front door where she rang the doorbell.

Along this street, on the other side, one of the houses stood out from the rest. It was a modern house in a street of dignified nineteenth-century buildings, and its façade jutted jaggedly outward. In 1970, the original house had been blown to pieces in an explosion. The house had been used as a weapons store and bomb factory by the ultra-leftist Weather Underground Organization. Bob Schofield had chosen to live in this street because he liked its connection with the sixties radicalism in which he had come of age, and in which the Narwhal Foundation had been born. In choosing to live here he was saying to the world, We may have had a setback then, but we're still here. Now these houses were worth their weight in caviar. And now, with Donna's news, Bob Schofield faced a new setback, one that could finish off Narwhal for good.

Bob Schofield opened the door, disregarding the gust of cold, wet wind blowing into him. He was bald, bearded, grey-haired, and wore a long black dressing gown. He took her bag, and ushered her into the house.

3

The door slammed shut. As they stood in the hallway, Bob Schofield said, 'Thanks for your message, Donna. Are you OK? How are you feeling?'

'I'm all right, I guess,' Donna said. 'It's still such a shock.'

'I can understand that. It's a shock for all of us,' Bob Schofield said. 'But thank you for coming. I know it's probably the last thing you want to do.'

He looked her up and down and said, 'My God, you need some warm clothes.'

'I didn't think I'd need them in Brazil,' she said. 'I didn't expect to be coming here.' While she was saying this, he turned and called up the stairs.

'Suzie!'

Suzie appeared, Mrs Bob Schofield or the equivalent, softly descending the carpeted staircase. She wore fine, shoulder-length hair, expensively cut and diaphanously highlighted, a grey cashmere sweater, a pearl necklace, and an utterly untroubled expression. She held out a tanned, slender hand to Donna. She seemed closer in age to Donna than to Bob Schofield. She had been upstairs writing an article on Alice Neel for *Artforum* magazine.

'Oh, your hand is so cold,' she said, in a kindly music. 'You poor thing. We're so glad you're here. I hope the journey wasn't too bad.'

The journey had been long and exhausting. But Bob Schofield was the kind of man who could summon someone from halfway around the world and they would come.

'Can she borrow something to wear?' Bob Schofield said. 'One of your big sweaters?'

Suzie appraised her size with a gently furrowed brow. Donna's small clothing size seemed more serious to her than the matter that had brought Donna here. 'All mine might be a bit too big for you. I'll have a look.'

Suzie went upstairs to see what she could find, and Bob Schofield led Donna into a large living room divided in two by folding doors. Faded antique kilims covered the wooden floor, the walls glowed an opulent red, and a Warhol portrait of Mao Tse-tung hung over the marble mantelpiece. She sat on a deep sofa by the front window. She had heard about this place: Bob Schofield's amazing house in New York City, where he ran the Narwhal Foundation, as well as his other businesses (software, movies, high-tech venture capital). He had an office upstairs, but the main offices of the Narwhal Foundation were in Seattle.

'Look. Why don't you stay for a while. There's a nice room upstairs.' He said it with elegant vagueness, as though the room were just lying around, as if it belonged to nobody in particular.

'Take a couple of days off and get some rest. Then we can talk, when you're ready. I want to know the whole story.'

'That sounds good,' Donna said. She felt abruptly ashamed of saying this: it was not the sort of expression she would normally use. She was about to cry when Suzie came back carrying an armful of clothes. Suzie stood tactfully in the doorway, waiting for a cue.

'Come on,' he said. 'I'll show you your room. Violetta will bring you some tea. I guess you're probably starving as well.'

She followed them up the stairs, to a small bedroom with a Federal Period bed covered with an antique quilt. The window looked onto the Greenwich Village street.

'We'll leave you alone for a bit,' Bob Schofield said, setting her bag on a chair by the window. 'Come down whenever you like.'

The door clicked shut. Donna immediately felt glad to be alone at last, and grateful for the sanctuary Bob Schofield offered her, far from Brazil, far from the ship, far from everything that had happened in the past terrible weeks. She fell onto the bed face down.

The next day, after a long sleep and a long bath in a deep bathtub, Donna sat on a chair by the window, looking out over the street on which snow was falling softly, muffling the sound of traffic, alone, warm and dry in a comfortable room in a strange, huge house. She was certain of one thing: to tell Bob Schofield this story in a way that made sense, she would have to begin with Seb: Seb was the beginning and the end of this story.

P. J. Gough

P. J. Gough was born in England but grew up in Africa. She trained as a nurse in Cape Town during the bitter and devastating years of apartheid before returning to England to pursue nursing in a more humanitarian and compassionate environment. Following many years working as a health visitor in and around Bristol she finally left clinical practice for a life in health policy analysis and health services development. She remains passionate about both nursing and the NHS. She is married and lives in north London.

This excerpt is from the first two chapters of her novel *Herbert and Edi*.

Herbert and Edi

Edi

My brother Herbie is standing outside my bedroom door. He's been there a while, now – just on the other side. I can hear the floorboards creaking under his feet. Once the door handle turned slowly, as if he would come in. I could have called out. But I weren't sure. So I'm laying here, holding my breath. Listening to him move about in the dark.

Now he's started down the stairs. He's treading quietly as he can. I can hear his hand rubbing against the other side of my wall as he goes down. Step by step. Feeling his way. I wish he would make some noise. Then I could ask him, 'What is it, Herbie?' It's not right. In the dark. Slowly I turn over and look hard at Mam's old clock on the table. I think it tells me three o'clock. I lie back against the pillows with my hand over my heart. His moving about has unsettled me.

At the bottom of the stairs the door latch clicks. I hear Herbie sighing – ever so soft – as he steps into the room below. I wonder if his feet are bare on that stone floor. It would be like standing on ice. When we were small those cold flags would chill us right up our legs. The floor was always warmer near the fire. That was the place to stand. Or on the rug Mam had made of knotted rags. That old rug is still there. Sometimes Herbie takes it into the garden to beat the dust out of it. I watch him from my window.

His feet make no noise now, being on the stone. But I knows just where he is. I can hear Mam's china cups clinking on their hooks. I sometimes think about those cups. So thin and light. You can see through them, like a shell held up to the window. I asked him just last week, 'Are Mam's china cups still down there, on the dresser?' He said, 'Of course, Edi. Where else would they be?'

Now he's at the window. I listen as he works the catches to open the shutters. He don't need to stand on the window seat to reach. Not like I used to. He hardly has to stretch. As a young man he were so tall his head it almost touched the ceiling in that room. And after he started quarrying he had a pair of shoulders on him, too. Like the dray horse that used to come past the cottage in the morning. Herbie were a brawler, mind. But no one in the village ever got the better of him. Even when he were too drunk to stand up. After Da had passed on, this was nearly all the time.

Herbie's stirring the fire. The noise, it's coming right up the chimney into my room. I can hear him talking to Cyril. He tells me that cat sleeps down there most nights. That's as much as he knows. Time was it would be out hunting all night. But now it comes onto my bed. We're all that old we don't stir past the door too often. Herbie does some shopping, that's all. I don't even go outside my room. But that don't mean I miss what's going on. Herbie brings me news from round and about. And if I look out of my window I can see how it's all changing. Across the valley to the town. We started off a village but now we're just part of Coalbourne town itself. All those new houses. One day Herbie will tell me we're joined up right the way to Bristol. And that used to be a whole twelve mile away. I went there a few times when I was a girl. Full of people, noise and cars. Now the village is full of cars too. They even come up and down The Dell. Right past the end of our garden. Herbie says you have to be careful stepping off our path, in case a car knocks you down. At one time, just the sound of a car would have us running outside to see it pass.

Suddenly, Herbie is in my room. I must have gone off again. His hand on the edge of the bed, that's what's woke me. I can't see his face too well, dimmed as it is in the dark. He must have heard me stir.

'Edi?'

His voice is soft, not hoarse like when he's been drinking. I lay still all the same.

'Edi, I've been thinking 'bout your leg.'

I can feel his breath on my face as he bends down low to look at me. A car comes up the hill. Even at this hour. The lights they catch the top of his head. I sees his face, sharp, between me and my ceiling. He steps back quick. The silence stays between us.

'Your poorly leg, Edi,' he says at last. 'He just don't look right to I. I've been fretting all night.' He stops and waits. 'Edi?'

I feel the sore place on my ankle start to burn, finding its own voice to nag at me. I move my leg to ease it. I have no heart to hear what Herbie has to say.

'Edi, I knows thee would rather I held my tongue. But I worry that you's got trouble brewing there, with your leg and all. I thought it would be for the best if . . .'

A sound rushes out of my mouth. Just as if he's knocked the wind out of my chest. It startles me to hear it out loud in the room.

Herbie catches my arm. 'Edi?' My mouth opens but the words, they don't come out.

'Well, what then?' he says at last and sighs, so long and sad. It tears me to hear him. 'What's to be done? I'm feared to leave it.'

I turn my head away to face the window and close my eyes. I wish that Herbie hadn't brought his fear into my room. I'm already tired with my own worry of it all. He's been fretting for just one short night. I've kept it hid since the start of the year. It wasn't much to see at first. Just a patch of skin the colour of coal above my ankle. It itched and shed angry scales like the scurf on a baby's head. I try not to scratch it. Sometimes the urge, it's too great. It prickles and flames like I'd touched it with an iron from the fire. It's the leaking of its juices onto the sheets that's drawn Herbie's prying eye. And its raw smell.

'Edi. Will thee tell I, what should I do?'

Herbie is fidgeting like a wasp at the window pane. I want no part of this. It will go away with time. That's the way it's always been with us.

'Edi, this be going round and round my head all night.'

I feel Herbie's weight shift from the bed head. He stands up tall and draws in his breath. I can hear the air whistling through his gizzard. He always tells bad news like this, from when he was a child. He would take a large breath of air and then land his blow – he'd killed a bird or torn his clothes or Da was in a fight.

'Right, if thee won't say then I'll tell thee what's what. I be going down to Dr Belgrave when his surgery opens later to ask him what to do.'

I can hear the shaking in his voice. The whimpering rises in my chest.

'He were kind, that Dr Belgrave, Edi, gurt kind to us when Mam died. And when I thought I needed help with you, those years back, he got they social people to come round . . . even though you turned them away.' Herbie's voice sounds broken. I can hear his breathing rattling in his chest.

'Edi . . . I'm not sure I can keep on with looking after you this way. Not now. Not with your leg and all.'

So there's nothing more to be said. We wait in the quiet. After a while Herbie sits down on the bed. I can hear him snivelling into his sleeve. I keep my face turned away. The light is creeping back into the room. I can see the bumps and patterns on my bedroom wall now. Slowly coming back, coming back. These comfort me against Herbie's words. Here's the dent where Emma threw her hairbrush in a fight with one of the others. I watched her through the bars of my cot. Over there, above the skirting, the kicks and scuffs of our black shoes. The wooden sill at the window is lifting with the damp. It shows a crack beneath its edge. A cold wind has blown through there these last few winters. The wall beneath is smooth. Polished by the clothes and bodies of my brothers and sisters as they pressed against it. A long time ago now. Washing, getting dressed, making beds, laughing and shouting. So many of us. And such a little room. Then there was the war and it was much quieter after that. They all went off here and there. My older brothers, they didn't make it home. All of them gone. But I still feels them here. In and out of the doors. Up and down the stairs. In the end it was just Mam and Herbie and me. And for a long time now it's been just Herbie and me. Out of all that noise and hurly-burly. Just the two of us left.

I turns to look at Herbie, grey in the morning light.

'If thee tells the doctor, Herbie. If they people come in here again. This time it will be the end for us.'

I see the fear written clear across his dear face. I find his hand, cold on the bedclothes, and hold it to my cheek. And after a while Herbie lays down next to me. I find comfort in his great, warm body against mine. I lies awake until full light and then Herbie rouses himself and leaves my room. He goes quick without looking back at me. Soon I hear him running water in the kitchen. I lays still and waits.

Herbert

It took me a while, I can tell you. One thing after another to hold me up. My razor blade was blunt. I hadn't bothered to heat any water and in the early light I couldn't see to shave. So, I ends up cutting a scrage along my chin which looked like I'd been done by a knifeman. Then I had to sponge down my suit to take off the mildew spots. It's been that long since I wore it last. I found a paper napkin in the pocket, so it must have been the funeral. Edi was still on her feet when Mam died and she did all these sandwiches and things.

After this I needed to press my trousers. I found the old iron behind all Edi's china in the dresser. Seeing all those lovely plates upset me, so I let it be.

I knew Edi would take it bad, about her leg. But I had to do something. She weren't going to do nothing off her own bat. She's not one to say outright when something needs doing. Oh, she's got a tongue on her to scold me. But it's what she don't say that I have to watch for. Like finding the mess on her sheets from her leg. That weren't no accident. Oh no. She let me find it, clever like, and then she waited. She knew I would do something. Get help. That's her way, see.

So, when I finally got out the door it was gone eight o'clock already. I walked as quick as I could up The Dell to the crossroads. Then I had to stop and catch my breath. As a boy I could run up here, right from the stream. But there it is. I had no choice but to lean against the railings on the edge of the road and wait for my chest to loosen up.

P. J. Gough

Twenty minutes, usually, to get into the town centre from The Down, but with all my stopping and starting I reckon it took me twice as long. That gave me a start. I hadn't counted on getting that slow since I was last over by the old hospital. I worked it out as I went along. Must be about five year gone. Not that it's a hospital now. Hasn't been for years. The doctors took it over long before any of the new houses were built. It's just their surgery these days. In its day, though, before the war, it was quite a busy place. It did all sorts. Operations. Tubercular. I was born there – 1920. Mam could have had me at home like the others but she said by the time I came along she wanted to be looked after and have a rest.

So I finally walks into the waiting room and my face must have been the colour of a beacon. The girl behind the desk, she asks me if I'm all right. I said, well if I'm not, I'm in the right place, aren't I? She didn't take much to that and told me to sit down. I was glad to do that by this time, mind, so I didn't argue. She was just a slip of a thing too. Time was I would have checked her back and got a smile out of her. But you need breath to do that and what with sounding like a steam engine, all puffing and panting, I just took my place. Meek as a lamb, me. Although if you were to ask Edi she might tell you different.

I didn't like being there, in the old hospital building. With all my worry about Edi, I had somehow kept this locked in the back of my mind. But once I was sat down it started to come back. It may be different now, with new bits added here and there, but it's still the same place, same smells. It was the waiting room ceiling that set me off. I just happened to look up and it all came back – the uneven borders at the corners and all that fancy plasterwork at the centre. I knew it off by heart. I had laid in here often enough staring up at it. And then before I knew it, I was thinking about Tommy. He had been here in the hospital that summer too, in the ward block on the far side. So many. All beaten up and bits lopped off. I didn't want to think about those things so I looked away quick, back to the girl behind the desk. My chest started to go tight and I felt I couldn't breathe. So I stood up and went outside to wait for Dr Belgrave. The girl at the desk didn't like it. I almost came home then. It was Edi kept me there.

When it was my turn Dr Belgrave came right outside to fetch me.

'Hello, Mr Tanner,' he says and holds out his hand. 'Come this way, please.' I followed him into his surgery. Well, he calls it his surgery but it was the same old room where they used to give us the injections all those years ago. I recognised it straight away, no messing. So I didn't feel very good all over again. We sat down and Dr Belgrave waits while I catch my breath. And when I finally manage to lift my head to look at him he's staring at me very hard. He leans forward, and looks at me over the tops of his glasses and he reaches out and puts his hand on my shoulder.

'Mr Tanner,' he says, very kindly, 'does this room bother you?' And I'm so surprised that he knows I just nods my head.

So he says, 'Well, that's no problem. Why don't we go into my colleague's office and use that? It's brand new – not part of the old place.' And off we go, out the back door, across a path and into another building.

I felt much better in the new bit, I can tell you. We sits down again and he runs a hand over his head to smooth his hair down. Not that he's got much. He puts his glasses back on the end of his nose. Dr Belgrave is no young 'un, maybe ten years less than me, but I can tell you I have more hair on my head than he has. You've aged, boyo, since I saw you last, I thought. He's never been a heavy weight but I fancied he was scrawnier than ever too. And he's my height. Like a long streak of nothing. He collar starts off his neck like a noose.

And then he says, 'Now, Mr Tanner, how can I help?' and do you know, I couldn't think of a word to say. I'd done all that talking with Edi and walked all that way and I hadn't even thought about what words to use. But Dr Belgrave wasn't fussed. He just sat there with his elbows on his desk and his hands under his chin, waiting till I got it sorted out.

'Edi,' I says at last. 'It's Edi. Her leg, it's got this sore on it. Had it for months and she hasn't said nothing to I all this time. Now it's just a gurt mess and I don't think I can look after her like this any more.'

I realised then what had come out and how I had said it and I looked down at my great big hands and they was shaking. So I held them together. And just to make sure I carried on looking down at them for a bit.

'Edi's your sister, isn't she?' Dr Belgrave says, real quiet. I nodded and didn't look at him because I was still keeping an eye on my hands. 'And how old is she now?'

I had to work it out. I were seventy-eight. 'She be nearly eighty-two, now,' I said. 'And she be in her bed on and off about fifteen year. She went off her feet after our Mam died.'

'And who looks after her, Mr Tanner?'

Well, what a question. So I says to him, 'Well, I do, Doctor. There ain't no one else. Except for they Meals on Wheels. But, no one else. It be just the two of us.'

Dr Belgrave looked at some notes on his desk.

'Yes, Meals on Wheels,' he says as if he just thought of it. 'I remember. That's when you came to see me last time – about five years ago?' He tapped the paper with they long thin fingers and looked over the tops of his glasses at me. 'We thought a bit of help might be needed then, didn't we? We asked social services to come and visit. Do you remember that?'

Do I remember? Edi went mad. Bolted herself in her room and shouted and shouted. So I says to him quick,

'I don't want no social people in again, thank you. Edi wouldn't let them in the door. Shook us up proper, I can tell you. I just want someone to sort out her leg.'

Dr Belgrave took off his glasses, then stands up and walks over to the window. He pulls on his ear lobe while he thinks.

'Mr Tanner . . .'

'Please call I Herbert,' I said. 'There ain't no one calls me Mr Tanner no more.'

'Herbert,' he says and he looks right at me again. 'I need to ask you what you really want me to do.'

Herbert and Edi

And Dr Belgrave, he says this real slow and serious, like. And it scares me this question. I looks down at my hands seeing as they're shaking again. I start to feel hot and strange.

'I told thee already, Doctor. I want someone to look at her poorly leg. If that were better then we'd be all right and we can go on as before.'

'And is that what you want to do, Herbert?' he says, his arms folded in front of him. 'To go on as before? It must be very hard for you.'

I decided then that I didn't have no more answers. So I pushes back my chair and stands up.

'I manages fine, thank you, Dr Belgrave,' I says. 'I've got to get back to Edi now.'

Dr Belgrave looked surprised then he smiles.

'Of course, Herbert. Look, I'll tell you what I'm going to do. I'm going to ask the nurse to come in and have a look at Edi's leg. I'll see if she can pop in this afternoon. Would that be all right? Good. And look, if you want to come back at any time, you know, to talk things over, you are very welcome. Any time.'

And with that he reaches over and shakes my hand again. He opens the door and shows me out. And I'm left outside, thinking, what is there to talk over? I've said all I had to say. So I puts my hat back on my head and starts off for home.

Nicholas Hollin

Blog is Nicholas Hollin's first novel. He has previously worked as a government researcher, an English teacher, and a forensic imagery analyst. He currently lives in Cambridgeshire. This excerpt is from chapter one of *Blog*.

Blog

Surprised? I am. I didn't think I'd ever do this again. I couldn't bring myself to close down the site, in case you came across it late, but I had no intention of posting anything new. I was happy enough knowing I'd given it my best shot, that I couldn't have done any more to try and convince you. I'm still happy knowing that, and I'm not writing this because I think it'll make any difference, it's just a hell of a lot's happened recently that I desperately need to tell you about. If I don't I know it'll only end up driving me mad.

I've also been thinking about something you told me. You told me that getting things down on paper was the only way you could get things straight in your head. I remember you saying that because I used to think that was one of the reasons why you hadn't come back. I imagined you out there somewhere, furiously typing away, writing down everything that went on with you and Sarah, trying to figure out why you did what you did. When you'd finished, when you'd got it all sorted, I thought you'd be ready to return.

I don't think that anymore, of course, there's only so long you can go on believing something like that, but what I am now thinking is that it might work for me, that writing everything down might help me to understand a little better.

I have a confession to make. I've read your manuscripts. We found them in a box in a wardrobe in your flat. But then if you didn't want us to read them you shouldn't have left them behind. Anyway, I mention that because I'm trying to decide where to start, and I'm wondering how you'd have started if you did try and write about Sarah. In your fiction you set off fairly upbeat and then slowly let the characters fall apart. I bet you found you couldn't do that when it came to writing about real life. I can't either. You see, if I were to start by telling you about how Emma and I met and how our relationship developed it would only make it harder for me to tell you how I fucked it all up. So I'm going to skip the happy stuff. I'm also going to miss out how the relationship ended because we'll need to come back to that anyway and it'll need an explanation and I'm not sure I can think of one yet. In fact, I reckon the best option for the time being is to try and forget about the confusion and complication of my relationship with Emma and concentrate on what happened with Peter.

Let me get a glass of water first. My throat is suddenly quite dry, and if I'm going to sit here for the next few hours hammering away at the keyboard I'll need something to drink. I would have something stronger, but it's only nine o'clock in the morning, and my drinking hasn't got that bad. I'll save the hard stuff for later in the day. It'll give me something to look forward to. Right, so I'll pop and fetch that water, and when I return I'll get on with the story. I won't be long. For you I won't be any longer than a single space down the page.

The pub where I first saw Peter was a shit-hole. It was one of the worst pubs I've ever been in, and I've drunk in some real dives over the past few years. From the outside it had looked okay – Victorian, terraced, red brick, rather stately – but when I got inside I remember laughing at how bad it was. Actually, when I first stepped inside I couldn't see very much, because although it was the middle of the afternoon on a bright winter's day, the windows were so filthy that very little light was getting in. The only thing I was immediately aware of was a fruit machine in the corner, which was flashing crazily and playing a tune that sounded like a funeral march. Or maybe that's just the way I remember it. When my eyes finally adjusted to the gloom, and when I started to wish they hadn't, I could also make out flowery, smoke-stained wallpaper, an equally flowery carpet, coated in dirt, beer and judging by the smell something worse, rickety wooden chairs, large rectangular wooden tables, a rusty electric fire in front of a bricked-up fireplace, an empty picture frame above that fireplace, a bracket for a telly but no telly, a specials board with nothing on it . . . I could go on, as sadly that place seems to have stuck in my mind, but I don't want to, because it's depressing, and there's not much point anyway, because I feel sure you know the kind of pub I mean. Indeed, for all I know you might have been to that very one yourself.

If you have been there I hope you were served quicker than I was. I had to wait for ages before the barman – tall, skinny, ponytail, tattoos, pierced nose, pierced ears, pierced tongue, pierced other bits quite possibly, but I'd rather not think about that – finally appeared from out the back, a copy of the *Racing Post* clutched in his hand, and asked me what I wanted.

'A pint of Fosters, please.'

'Are you old enough?'

'Old enough for what?'

'Old enough to drink here.'

'Looking at the décor, probably not.'

'Don't get smart with me.'

'It's hard not to.'

'What did you say?'

'I said I'm twenty-two,' I lied. I was twenty-one at the time. I was twenty-two last Monday, in case you'd forgotten, and you must have forgotten because I didn't get a card.

'You don't look twenty-two,' the barman continued, peering down at me. 'You look like a child.'

'Well, I'm not. I told you, I'm twenty-two. Now stop being an arse and get me a beer.'

'Call me an arse again and the only thing you're gonna get is a smack in the face.'

'You wouldn't hit a child, would you?'

I was drunk, clearly not so drunk that I couldn't speak, just drunk enough to risk getting myself into trouble. Not that I did get into trouble, at least not with the barman, because he suddenly started to laugh, revealing the piercing on his tongue I mentioned before, and pulled me a pint without saying another word, other, that is, than to ask me for three pounds eighty. It was at least thirty pence more than I should have paid, I was well aware of that, but then after a sudden attack of conscience about how rude I'd been to the guy, an attack of conscience that happened to coincide with him threatening to hit me, I wasn't about to argue.

When I finally sat down with my hard-earned pint I looked over to the left and spotted a man at a table in the corner. Under the table in front of him was a dog. The man was dressed in a dark grey reefer jacket, a blue knitted sweater, and a pair of old jeans. His hair was thick and dark and messy, as was his beard, which covered the whole of the lower half of his face. He looked like a trawler boat fisherman, or at least how I imagine they should look, and funnily enough whenever I glanced across at him I could see his head swaying from side to side as though he was having trouble getting used to being back on dry land. Not that a pub should be considered dry land.

I wondered if it might have been you at first, when I saw a tall, slim, middle-aged man looking drunk and miserable in the corner. I do that sometimes, where I end up staring at people if anything about them looks familiar. Occasionally I might even follow them around for a bit until I know for sure that it isn't you. And it isn't easy to be sure because I don't really know what you look like now.

Don't think you're special being followed. I've been following a few people's looky-likeys recently, down back streets, through parks, through shopping centres, on and off buses, into dodgy pubs. That makes me sound like a weirdo, but read the rest of this and you'll understand.

Anyway, the guy in the pub wasn't you, it was Peter, the Peter I mentioned at the start, and the Peter I'll be mentioning at the end. I can't give you a more detailed description of him, because I never really looked that hard. In fact, apart from that first time, when I was making sure he wasn't you, I was mostly trying to avoid looking at him.

Describing the dog is far easier. And not only because when I was avoiding looking at Peter I'd normally end up looking at her, but because she's sitting here with me now, curled up under the desk as I write this, keeping my feet warm. All I have to do is push my chair back a little, making sure her tail isn't under one of the wheels, and . . .

Winnie's a border collie. She's basically black on top and white underneath – when she hasn't been wading through puddles in the park or rolling in the mud patch that's supposed to be my garden. She also has a narrow white blaze running between her eyes, a thick white band round her neck, and a dollop of white on her nose and at the end of her tail. The most distinctive thing about her is that she's 'wall-eyed', which means one of her eyes is brown and the other pale blue. That pale blue eye, which I can't see at the moment because she's fast asleep, is incredibly beautiful. It is also a little disconcerting sometimes, because it stares so intently, or at least appears to, that I start to worry about what she's thinking. And I have good reason to worry about what she's thinking given that she was a witness to almost everything I'm about to tell you.

I've only had Winnie a month and a half, but I'm already very attached to her. It's taken me a while to get used to having to walk her three times a day: first thing in the morning, during my lunch break (I have to pop home from work), and last thing at night; and it's costing me a fortune in food, because she's got a phenomenal appetite; and I've been woken a few times by her snoring (she sleeps in a basket at the bottom of the bed), but I'm glad she's here to keep me company. I'd forgotten how much I like having a dog around the house. Actually, it's funny, because occasionally when I get home from work and I'm not thinking, or I'm thinking about something else, I'll mistakenly call out for Jess.

You remember Jess. You must remember her better than I do. You were the one that chose her in the first place, when we went to that farm in Shropshire or wherever it was and you picked ahead of all the others her because she wouldn't stop following us around. And you used to take her for long walks through the woods behind the house, sometimes not coming back for hours so that mother would start to worry. You must also remember how she'd always come and greet us with something in her mouth, like a shoe or a sock or a newspaper or even one of those ridiculous squeaky toys that mother used to buy for her.

Jess is dead. She died three years ago. I hadn't seen her very much for a couple of years before that so I suppose I coped with her death better than I ever thought I would when I was living at home and seeing her all the time. Back then I didn't know what I was going to do when she died. I thought it was going to be the same as when you disappeared and I didn't want to have to go through that again.

Her death hit the parents the hardest. It was father who rang to say they'd had to have her put down and as you know father's always hated using the phone. It also took him ages to tell me. He kept asking me questions about what I was up to and how I was doing, so I already knew there was something wrong. I think that's why when he did finally break the news I was the one that ended up saying it was for the best and she'd had a good life and fourteen was a bloody good age for a dog. When I'd said all that and when we'd hung up not long after, I remember wishing I'd appeared more upset, because I was upset and I would have liked father to know that.

If you're wondering why I haven't told you about Jess's death before it's because I didn't think you deserved to know. The way I looked at it, if I couldn't know about you, if I couldn't know if you were alive or not, why the hell should you get to know about her?

I'm willing to tell you now for a number of reasons, not least because you'll have already worked it out for yourself. She was ten when you left. And if she were still alive today she'd be seventeen, which is far too old for a Labrador . . . Having said that, you might have done some research on the Internet, because I know (and I'm counting on it) that you became obsessed with the Internet before you left, and you might have discovered, as I've just discovered, that the oldest Labrador in the UK lived for twenty-seven years! But then even if you did you wouldn't have been stupid enough to think Jess would last that long. No, I'm sure if you'd wanted to see her again, before it was too late, you'd have come home ages ago.

That's the other reason I didn't tell you Jess had died, of course. I didn't want to give up any possible reason for you returning. I thought you'd still miss her if you were out there on your own, the way I sometimes missed her when I got back to wherever it was I was living and there was nobody there to greet me. Even when you must have known she was old, perhaps too old to be alive, I hoped you'd still come back to check on her.

I suppose it's possible that you did come back at some point, because you could easily have sneaked into the parents' garden or into the house when they were out (they've never changed the locks). In which case, mother might have been right about objects in the house being moved. I never believed her, because I couldn't see why you'd need to disturb anything, unless you wanted us to think you'd been back, unless you were trying to haunt us, but even if it wasn't you, even if it was just another example of mother's mind playing tricks, I'd still like to think you found a way to see Jess at least one more time before she died, because I know that dog really cared about you.

It's sad with dogs how quickly you can replace them. That's not to say I don't think about Jess from time to time; as I say, I do occasionally call out her name when I'm distracted, and I always think about her when I go to visit the parents, but now I've got Winnie, now I've got someone else to greet me when I get home from work, I find I think about her much less. Winnie doesn't bring me stuff like Jess used to, probably because there's hardly anything in this flat for her to bring, but she does always come bounding across with her tail wagging furiously and that always cheers me up, no matter how shitty my day might have been, and no matter that every time I see her I'm reminded of how she ended up here.

Winnie's tail wasn't wagging the first time I saw her. But then she was sitting on a stinking carpet in a stinking pub with a stinkingly drunk owner, so it's hardly surprising. She was also tied to a table leg with an old piece of rope. I imagine she was used to sitting like that, having, as I later discovered, spent most of the previous month in a similar position, but it still upsets me when I think of her tied to a table leg, especially as the rope wasn't even long enough to allow her to stretch out fully. And it wasn't as though Peter needed to tie her up. She's not the sort of dog to go running off anywhere, at least she's never tried with me, and I was the only other person in the pub – even the barman had disappeared again – so there weren't many distractions. I guess Peter wanted to make absolutely sure he wasn't going to lose her, which is odd when you consider what he was planning to do next. But then I'm getting ahead of myself.

I have no idea how long I sat in that pub looking across at Peter and Winnie. I do remember thinking it wasn't nearly long enough for someone to drink four pints of beer. And yet that's exactly what Peter did, one after the other, pausing only occasionally to take a drag on a cigarette. His drinking wasn't even interrupted by having to go over to the bar, because he'd lined all four pints up in front of him. Add to those four pints the five empty glasses already pushed to one side of the table and it was an impressive effort. Personally, my limit has always been around the six-pint mark. I've never understood how people can stomach any more than that. I suppose like most things in life it gets easier with practice, and Peter certainly had practised. Then again so have I. But he was also tall, and tall people do tend to be better at handling their alcohol. I couldn't tell you how tall Peter was, by the way, not to any degree of accuracy, probably because in the time that I knew him he was hardly ever able to stand up straight. If I had to guess I'd say he was ten inches taller than I am. That would have made him six foot three.

I'm five foot five, in case you were struggling to work that out. I didn't grow a single inch after you left. In fact, I've hardly changed at all physically – hence the problem with barmen. I've got the same side parting and floppy fringe. I haven't put on any weight. I haven't put on any muscle. I still only shave once a week. I still dress like a 'fogey', in tailored shirts and corduroy trousers. This must be useful information if you've been following people around thinking they might be me. It must also be useful if you've been avoiding people for the same reason.

In all the time I sat looking at Peter he never once looked up, and when he tipped his head back to finish off another pint he always had his eyes closed. Even if he had looked across I doubt he'd have been able to focus enough to make me out. I imagine the first time he knew anything about me, therefore, other than when I was arguing with the barman (and he may not have heard much of that because he was sitting quite close to the fruit machine) was when he got up to leave and when I suddenly called out to warn him to be careful. I did so because I'd spotted that his coat sleeve was close to knocking one of the empty pint glasses off the edge of the table and I was worried Winnie might get injured. It wasn't that I thought she would be hit by the glass – she was sitting on the other side from where it would have fallen – it was that she was still tied to the leg of the table and the sound of something landing and possibly smashing on the ground behind her could easily have made her panic and try to run away. So I shouted out across the pub to warn him to stop. And he did stop. He stopped moving immediately. From the expression on his face I think he might have stopped breathing as well.

It was only later that I came to realise why he'd looked so confused by my calling out to him like that, and why he had looked so relieved – if relieved is the right word – when I called out for the second time and pointed to the glass by his left arm and when it suddenly dawned on him that I wasn't trying to stop him from doing what he'd thought I was trying to stop him from doing. I would certainly have tried to stop him from doing that as well had I known. But then I'm getting ahead of myself again.

Michael Hughes

Michael Hughes was born and raised in Northern Ireland, and now lives in London. *Towards Dawn* is an excerpt from his first novel.

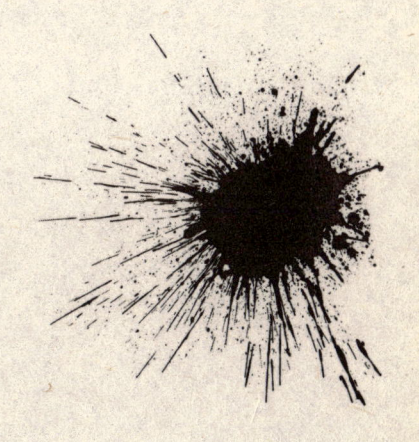

Towards Dawn

Five in the morning, and I hadn't slept a wink. I always had trouble in an unfamiliar bed, even with the comforting presence of a snoozing lover beside me; but alone, a sleepless night seemed endless, each blank minute longer than the one before. My naked skin was prickly with sweat. The bed was warm and my eyes were heavy, but the brain behind them just wouldn't switch off, buzzing itself into a swarm of useless nuisance. There was so much I had to think about, but nothing would come into focus. All I wanted was silence, and peace, and sleep; but the constant sounds of the nighttime world outside were grinding their way into my head, and there was nothing I could do to stop them.

I had known it would take time to get used to the nocturnal life of a new locale, but after twelve long nights my insomnia appeared to be getting worse. The road below my window seemed as busy as in daytime, and the rattling plate glass kept little of it out. No voices at this hour, but steady traffic humming past. And rising across it, the sucking whine of a council vehicle clearing the gutters. Its rush of noise blotted out all else as it passed beneath; then it faded, moving on, and the normal rhythm of the street was restored. I knelt up for a look, craning my gaze down three storeys. Cars drifted by on the wet tarmac, and now I could see them, their regular swishing passage, like waves breaking on a pebbly beach, began to soothe me. They seemed ghostly, insubstantial things, existing only for the moments I perceived them. A burst of siren bleated out, and I found myself picturing seagulls, urgent and clamorous, wheeling in on discarded food. I closed my eyes, and I could imagine the streetlit sheen of the road like an evening sea, the textured surface lit from above by a dim wash of sunset orange. Then the sound of a larger vehicle dispelled the fantasy, and I blinked my eyes open: a nightbus, its heavy engine audible for a second above the slushy hiss of tyres on a rainy road, and a dying fall in its voice as it made a reluctant stop at a red light. The crossing bleeped emptily, as though to let some prowling phantom pass back to its cosy grave before sunrise. I heard the growling throb as the engine idled; then the orange signal glowed its permission, and the bus roused its burden of drowsy strangers into motion once more.

I abandoned the charade. I wasn't going to sleep tonight, and I tried not to care. I stood, stretched my legs and arms a few times, and padded across to the sink. My numb fingers plucked a teabag from its dusty packet, almost empty, and dropped it into a rinsed-out mug. I watched as traces of water in the bottom spread a wet stain through the flimsy paper, then shook the kettle and heard a sufficient slosh to risk switching it on without refilling. Within seconds it had reached a seething frenzy, the element fizzing with complaint at the lack of fluid. I tipped it up and boiling water streamed out and filled the mug, darkening as it rose. The last drips plopped in, an inch from the brim: I'd judged it right, and this tiny vindication cheered me. A splash of milk turned the amber liquid cloudy, then thickly opaque. I poked at the little bag with a teaspoon, then hoist it out and let it drop into the rubbish-stuffed plastic bag at my feet. A drip of hot tea from the spoon stung my naked foot, and the moment of tingling pain was enough to spoil my brightening mood. I slunk back to bed, disgruntled; but already my little cocoon had lost its heat, and however much I pulled the thick duvet to myself I couldn't recreate the dozy comfort I'd left just a minute before.

I had to eke out such minor pleasures and disappointments these days. A cup of tea could be major punctuation to the day, and a suddenly cold bed a significant crisis. My world had shrunk down to just this new flat and the mini-row of shops across the road: a Costcutter supermarket, a Chinese takeaway, a shabby florist, and two pubs. These last I hadn't dared enter: one looked like the sort of place where conversation stopped if at least half the clientele didn't know your first name, while the other was an optimistic stab at Shoreditch cool in which I had never seen a single drinker. I couldn't tell if the For Sale sign meant it had just opened, or was about to close. It was a dingy part of town, charmless and aggressively downmarket, but I knew now I'd been lucky to find somewhere tolerable to live alone on my budget. The studio flat was warm and clean, functional and convenient, but tiny compared to my old place. It was not the first I had looked at; a couple had been damp, smelly, and a disgrace for the price demanded. All I really needed was central heating and a decent shower, was that too much to ask? Dispirited, I grabbed the first I thought I could just about bear to see when I woke up every morning. One room, almost filled by the steel-frame bed, with a tiny desk and rickety chair in one corner and a double-plate electric hob and microwave on the thin formicaed worktop, under which stood a grubby fridge and washing machine. Plus a cramped cubicle housing loo and shower, unhygienically close, though at least both pumped water with satisfying pressure. Fake wood flooring, cheap chromed plastic fittings, a few tacky angled lamps in the ceiling: it was a flat-pack parody of what I had left behind, and still extraordinarily poor value for money. One hundred and five pounds per week, more than I'd been paying on my mortgage, but which mercifully included the punitive local Council Tax. That left other expenses, perhaps as much again, to my own resources. With a ten thousand pound overdraft and no money coming in, I had a year at most to sort myself out, if I didn't spend too much on flummery.

But it was a hard habit to break. I had already added a kettle, a toaster, a blender, a juicer, and an espresso maker, what I considered the bare essentials of a civilised existence. They were clustered together, a kitchen jigsaw which only just fitted on the available surface. A chopping board on top of the microwave was my preparation area, and the single cupboard heaved with brand new pots, pans, steamers, colanders, graters and mixing bowls. So far, I hadn't used any of them. My credit card was bleeding, but none of the pricey gadgets had even been plugged in. For the first time in years I had to watch what I spent, and the mild despair that raised in me sent me straight for the sticky comfort of take-away menus. But to my surprise, these proved no more expensive per meal than the farmers' markets and delis I had patronised before. Buying fresh food usually meant at least half of it went in the bin: stale bread, wilting leaves, wrinkled fruit, browning meat. Afraid of having too little, I had always bought too much, and then threw away as much as I consumed. I used to have friends who claimed they couldn't bear to waste food, that they froze their leftovers and bagged and tagged them for future use. But I never saw the point: the joy of cooking for yourself, in a city, at the start of the twenty-first century, was the freedom to follow a whim, not to make yourself a slave to last month's impulse buys. Waste was a natural result of abundance. If there was ever a famine in London I would freeze for England, but until that day, I would buy what I wanted and do what I wanted with it. I felt no moral turpitude in letting food rot; I was too aware of the economics of its production to feel it made the slightest difference. In any case, the whole fragile edifice was built on people like me: if I threw away yesterday's fish, I would buy another lot today. Multiply that by the tens or hundreds of thousands of similar folk, and a few pounds of fresh fish not bought while you defrost some unloved stew makes a big hole in the profits of the supermarkets. If they start to sink, the suppliers and producers start to sink too. Then people are out of work, and they can't afford to buy so much, they too start to freeze their leftovers and the cycle gets worse: interest rates rise, house prices drop, the stock market plummets, the papers scream, governments panic, wars break out, the whole thing goes to shit. As long as the bins are full, the economy is healthy. At least, that's what I'd always been told.

I slurped at the lukewarm tea and watched faint light creeping in around my curtains; the night was ending, hip-hip-hooray. But all I could see ahead was another day spent digging away at myself, at the person I used to be. I was raking over this sort of thing compulsively now, exploring years of piled up second-hand opinions to see if I actually had any of my own. I had plenty of time to think these days, when I wasn't reading. I ignored the papers. Mercifully, I had no television, not even a radio. And what amazed me was that I didn't miss them in the slightest. In retrospect, the latter was much worse: constant smug chatter filling your head with unwanted facts and aspects, soundbites and statistics passed back and forth while boorish interviewers threw pretend-tantrums unworthy of infants. The myth of rolling news exposed as the same old lazy half-truths repeated every few minutes, self-important middle-aged blowhards pretending to know something about everything as they picked at each other's scabs. At least television was sometimes fun. Explosions and corpses from abroad held a visceral thrill that some droning expat sot could never hope to convey, however much he trotted out the usual tired rubbish about *bloodied survivors* and *the stench of death* from his five-star hotel rooftop. And the internet was worst of all. Sure, email was useful, but not if you were trying to avoid everyone you'd ever known. Apart from that, it was just innumerable screenfuls of brainless guff, which might as well have been written by the same four losers: a news wonk, a sex maniac, a gossipy old woman and a teenage conspiracy nut. There was nothing useful on there you didn't already know, or couldn't find in a decent encyclopaedia in half the time. And for the journalist, already the most lazy and unscrupulous fellow you could ever hope to meet, it just meant he could start and finish the 'story' without ever leaving his bedroom. Trust me, I used to do it myself.

Reading novels seemed to ease the hum of tension I constantly felt in my skull. A few days in here, I had made a stack of unread gifts, twenty at least, going back years, and I was about halfway through the seventh. I'd got out of the habit since living in London, and I was grateful for the relapse. The book was a terrific invention. A slab of words, thousands of them, feeding me the wisdom and experience of another, at my own pace, in silence. People I had never met whispering in my brain, leading me through a story they felt I ought to own. Fictions that made sense of the mindless, stupid world out there. Reassuring, comforting. Troubling sometimes, but only with a purpose. Of course some were bad, hard to get through, but even those I found impossible to discard unfinished. And there was always something, even just one nugget of insight or information, that made me glad I'd taken the trouble. And that they had, too.

Michael Hughes

My eyes scanned the clutter of the little room again. I'd been worried my sanity might slip away cooped up in here, but perhaps it was actually returning. This slough of self-absorption, not my style at all, at least freed me from the old tyranny of having to know things. I knew nothing now. The ice caps could have melted, the rain forests been cleared, the cows all died of bird flu and a cure been found for AIDS and I wouldn't be any the wiser. Maybe the Prime Minister had run off with a soap star. Perhaps the Archbishop of Canterbury had come out as gay. Maybe both were forgotten, with new men in the jobs. Why did I need to know? Would it make a difference to the weather? Would it change me back to who I used to be?

But I was beginning to question if that was really what I wanted after all. For the first time in my life, I wasn't sure I liked myself very much. At least, who I used to be. I thought I was probably a bit of an arsehole. I used to obsess about all that media stuff: the trivia of politics, the minutiae of scandal. Now, I wondered what sort of person could actually give a damn. It had been part of my job, of course, but I was always frantic to know the latest twists before the next man, to be the grinning bearer of bad tidings to the office. When a big shocker broke, I would send out a stream of gloating texts to friends, relatives, people I hadn't seen in months; once even to some Canadian chick I'd attempted a few nights before in a bar, charmed enough or pissed enough to entrust me with her number, but principled enough to leave it at that on first acquaintance. I felt a little rush of shame now as I remembered how the quirky name, Harmony, had suddenly tempted me from among the familiar list on my phone, an impression of her pouty face and singsong voice floating back with it. I knew I wanted her. So when the other texts were off, flattering myself she might be pining for me too, I doctored the exclusive with a few personal touches especially for her. The jokey intimacy of the message was supposed to trick her into thinking I might have a special little crush on her, rather than just a persistent itch in the crotch. The result was the expected, a hesitant 'Who is this?' which I volleyed back with mock-shock that she didn't remember; and then the gentle harassment began, a series of three or four over the morning in which I recalled flirty details, planted at the time to make sure she would talk about me next day to her buddies: an expensive cocktail bought, an outrageous bit of invented gossip about her favourite celeb, an extravagantly kooky compliment about her wobbly upper arms, the one bit of her body it was obvious she couldn't stand. And then, instead of a text back, she called, clearly very keen, my God of course I'm so sorry, blah blah, and we met up again that night or the next, and since nothing better turned up through the evening – for her as much as for me, I wasn't all that vain – we hit the sack at my place. She was quite a performer, I seem to remember, but not really my type. Or so I told myself. Somehow, I never got round to asking if I was hers.

I hugged the duvet tighter to myself, and wondered if I would ever share this new bed with another. A sleazy, complicit one-night stand was a guilty pleasure I had allowed myself rarely; at least in the last few months, after my relationship with Petra almost killed the desire for sex completely. Ah yes, Petra. My one significant adult girlfriend, but sometimes I thought if I could go back, I'd make sure I never met her. Petra the obsessive. Petra the depressive. Petra the messed-up, flipped-out, one-woman thrill-ride. More fun than a bag of puppies, as long as you didn't mind cleaning up the shit left behind. Crying, screaming, plotting, scheming, spying, lying, you name it, she had it up her sleeve. On a good day, I felt like I'd won the jackpot. She was smart, funny, sexy, horny, fiercely loyal to me when she thought I deserved it, and always independent. I knew about her little snogs when my back was turned, and I didn't mind too much, as long as it stayed at that. I'd had my moments too. But when she had a mood, or when I put her in one, it was warfare. Shock and awe. More fool me, for betting the house on a German. I'm sure I deserved it on occasion, but that didn't mean I had to come home to it for weeks at a stretch. Once she actually left a turd in my bed, concealed beneath the duvet, which I fortunately found seconds before I slid my bare feet into it. I wrapped it in the sheet and threw the lot in the bin. In her defence, that was the week I had shagged her eighteen-year-old cousin, a hormonal tornado visiting from Leipzig, who got through quite a number of her male friends, and a couple of the girls too. And in my defence, we were days away from the final break-up at the time, and the infidelity was a symptom, not the cause. But yes, I knew it would upset her, and yes, it worked. And I hadn't seen or heard from her since we split. No half-measures with Petra.

The awful cramp I'd had this morning was back, deep in my belly. And with it, another ache: a knot of emotion, heating and tightening in my chest. I hadn't thought so much about her in months. I wondered if she ever thought of me; if she ever had nights like this, when the past caught you unawares and flashed back into life. And as the memories clamoured for attention, I tried to focus on our first meeting: her quizzical half-smile at my increasingly frantic flirting, my heart juddering at my ribs in a way it hadn't since school, hoping she could find the space to fit me into her life, instead of the usual idle wondering if I'd got any room in mine. Would I still have gone ahead if I'd known what was to come? Did I really have any choice? I couldn't face going over it all right now. Pointless. I heard my stomach gurgle: the cramp had eased a little, but my chest was still hot and tight. The mug was cold in my hand, and I pressed it against my sternum, hoping the smooth coolness might creep inside. It numbed the skin, at least.

I felt like I might sleep at last. I set the mug on the floor and leaned back on the pillow, squeezing my eyes shut to get rid of Petra's image, but hoping somewhere darkly that I never fully did. If only we could have stayed in that first moment, our knees almost touching in the little back room at work where rival magazines sat piled by games consoles, action figures, DVDs, stacks of the stuff we were sent for free but never quite got round to looking at. Her gorgeous eyes, green and clear and huge. If I could just get to keep her eyes, pop them under my pillow to stare into when I was feeling blue. And the first tingling touch of her lips on mine, that explosive moment you spent every night for weeks after trying to recreate.

If I could slip that in my mouth and suck on it like a sweet. That would be the drug for me.

My body jolted, a spasm of almost-sleep that jerked my eyes open. I wasn't sure if I had actually dozed, but I was wide awake now. I stood suddenly, stretched again, and felt a dizzy rush of blood to my head. I rubbed my eyes, picked out a clump of yellow sleep, and looked outside. The sky was getting light, the traffic was picking up. Seven o'clock. The world was waking. The questions of the night swarmed around me again, but I swatted them away; for the moment, at least.

I knew one thing: I wouldn't find the answers in this room.

J. A. Lake

J. A. Lake moved to Britain in 1999 from the United States, where she trained as a cognitive neuroscientist. *Associations* is an excerpt from her novel-in-progress, *The Night House*, for which she received the Random House Fellowship in 2005/6. She lives and works in London.

Associations

My father was alone when he collapsed. No one was there to help him but his dog. All the doors were closed, and the dog couldn't get out of the house. My father was on the floor, unconscious, his head in the kitchen and his feet in the hallway, as she sniffed and dug the linoleum and circled frantically around him. She ran back and forth between the living room and the kitchen, barking at the front windows and clawing the doorknob and then going back to my father and licking his face. Eventually, much later, Mrs Hollis from across the street heard the barking. When she opened the door, she found the dog next to my father's body in the hallway, curled up in a puddle of urine, trembling, with a thick white foam around her lips. The dog had barked herself hoarse. Mrs Hollis tried to go to my father, but the dog lunged at her with bared teeth and sent her running back out of the house. When the paramedics arrived, they had to take the dog down with pepper spray and a rope before they could carry my father's body out.

I was at work when the call came from the hospital. I was working in the dark, in my office at the university, staring at the computer screen. I didn't know what time it was. There had been no definite end to the day; the sky had faded from white to grey to black sometime in the afternoon, and I had lost track of the hours after that. Everyone else in the building had gone home. I was trying to start a grant proposal. The chair of the department had taken me aside earlier in the week to warn me about the progress of my research, and suggested, firmly, that I make more of an effort to obtain external funding. He had conveyed this information in the flat, uncompromising manner of a person who performs experiments on rats. Sitting at my desk, I could see his face, the irritated trembling of its fleshy folds. The cursor flashed on the empty page. When the phone rang, the sound was as sudden and painful as a slap.

'We think your father's had a stroke,' said the voice on the other end. A young voice, like one of my students.

'Oh,' I said.

The voice didn't say anything for a short time. I wasn't sure whether I was expected to speak. I tried to pull myself away from the image of the department chair's face.

'He was admitted about half an hour ago. He's been in and out of consciousness, and we've been monitoring his vital signs. He's been sent for a CT scan, to confirm what we suspect and to determine the extent of the damage to the brain. We'll need to see the scan before we decide how to go ahead with treatment.'

I repeated the words to myself, silently, trying to make them attach to something sensible. I rubbed my face with my hand.

'How did you find this number?' I asked.

'Your father's neighbour came in with him. She found the number in his address book.'

I breathed deeply.

'Should I come in to the hospital?'

'You should probably be around when the results of the CT come in. I'm assuming you'll want to be here if he goes into surgery.'

'Oh. Yes,' I said.

After I hung up the phone, I shut the computer down. I waited for my eyes to adjust to the darkness.

The hospital was bright and confusing, buzzing with harsh bluish light. It was not one of the hospitals I visited regularly to find patients for research studies and was therefore unfamiliar and full of strangers. I felt grateful for this. A tiny, distracted woman in a pink uniform directed me to Critical Care. The automatic doors opened, and the cooler air from the ward moved across my skin and raised the hairs on my arms.

The doctor was clean-shaven and good-looking in a generic, sexless sort of way. I imagined he was accustomed to having women view him as an object of desire, although I did not, and I wanted to tell him so. He led me into an empty exam room and held the CT scan up to the light.

'This is a picture of your father's brain. It's sort of like an X-ray,' he said brightly.

I could feel the blood in my own head, throbbing. The image on the film was a series of greyish, white-rimmed ovals, each with a black butterfly shape in the centre: a skull and brain, in cross-section. My father's skull and brain. I had seen similar ovals many times, evaluating neurological cases for work. On one of the larger slices, I could make out a region that was lighter than the rest.

'Your father has had a haemorrhagic stroke,' said the doctor. 'An artery in his brain has ruptured. He's having surgery now to relieve the pressure and stop the bleeding.'

I nodded. I closed my eyes. I could see the after-image of the slices of brain, repeated in blue and poorly defined, against the backs of my eyelids.

'There is a very good chance he will come through the surgery.'

The doctor was putting on his blandest, most reassuring medical voice. I looked at him. He reminded me of the medical students I had encountered when I was in graduate school: smug, overconfident, impervious. I imagined him walking out of the hospital at the end of his shift, and putting his arm around a young nurse. I imagined him mentioning my father's case, offhandedly, as they lay beside each other in bed. I wanted to take his coat with both hands, and shake him. *Now, you're not being fair, you should give him a chance to help you.* My mother's voice. I rubbed my eyes with my fingers and sighed.

'Is there anything you'd like to know?' he asked.

I looked up at the scan. The light region was large.

'He won't be able to speak,' I said.

The doctor smiled patiently at me.

'We don't know how long your father was unconscious before he was discovered,' he said. 'In these cases, a lot depends on how soon a person is treated after the bleeding starts. I'm afraid we can't say at this point what the long-term outcome will be.'

I touched the scan, tracing the edge of one of the slices, next to the light region.

'Left inferior frontal,' I said. 'Classic speech area. He won't be able to speak.'

His eyebrows lifted.

'Are you a doctor?'

'I'm a neuropsychologist,' I said. 'Not clinical. Academic. I teach a course on language disorders at State.'

He tilted his head to one side as if trying to view me from a different angle, as if I possessed another dimension he hadn't noticed at first.

'You should have told me,' he said. 'This must be very strange for you.'

I looked back at him.

'Yes,' I said. 'My father might have died.'

I called my sister from the bank of pay phones just outside the main waiting area.

'I'm at the hospital,' I told her. 'Dad's had a stroke.'

I could hear her breathing on the other end.

'Kim?' I said.

'What?'

'Did you hear what I said?'

'I heard you,' she said. 'And?'

I rubbed my forehead. It was late, and I was alone in the hallway. I stood with my back to the pay phone, to avoid seeing my reflection in the metal.

'He could have died,' I said.

She sniffed.

'Well, maybe he should have stopped putting butter on donuts.'

I took a deep breath and swallowed. My throat was dry, and my eyes felt gritty and sore. I looked around for a place to sit down, but there was only the shelf under the phone, which wasn't wide enough. I leaned up against it. It caught my back in an uncomfortable place.

Associations

'It wasn't that kind of stroke,' I said.

'Whatever. Look, is there a point to this?'

'I thought you should know. I mean, I thought you'd want to know.'

'Okay. Now I know.'

'I thought you might come down to the hospital.'

She laughed.

'I think we both know *that's* not going to happen.'

'Can you just think about what I'm telling you? Something serious has happened here.'

'It's called justice,' she said.

I listened as she hung up.

I put the handset back into the cradle and walked over to the waiting area. It occurred to me that I hadn't eaten much since lunchtime, and I felt woozy and disoriented. I sat down on one of the long benches and put my head between my knees. The carpet was greenish grey, which didn't help. Someone put a hand on my shoulder. I looked up into the face of an older woman, who was smiling mildly.

'Stella Hollis,' she said. 'I live across the street from your father. I found him.'

I stared at her without saying anything. She had a pleasant face, homely and creased, and long silver hair. She patted my arm.

'You're going through a tough time,' she said. 'Is he still in surgery?'

'I think so,' I said, blinking at her.

'I can stay around until he comes out, if you like.'

'Oh. You don't have to do that.'

'All right, if you say so. I'll go home in a little while. Is there anything I can do for you while I'm here?'

I thought about thanking her for taking my word for it and agreeing to leave. My mother, for instance – before she left for good – would have argued with me, would have assumed that I wanted the company and was just being polite.

'Can you tell me what happened?' I asked.

She told me about my father, unconscious on the floor, and the dog. She told the story without making too much of her own part in it, which I admired.

'If the dog hadn't been barking, I wouldn't have gone over.'

'I wouldn't have gone over, either,' I said.

She nodded.

'What's happened to the dog?' I asked.

'The vet down the road has agreed to keep her for a week or so. Any longer than that and she'll be sent to the pound.'

I realized that I would have to go to the vet and pick up my father's dog. I felt terribly tired.

'Do you mind if I stretch out here?' I asked. 'I just want to close my eyes for a minute.'

'Of course,' she said. 'I'll go now.'

I watched her walk down the green corridor and out the sliding doors. The air in the room stirred, and then was still. I lay down on the bench, to wait.

'Surely you don't believe that there can be thought without language. Thought *is* language.'

It was Thanksgiving, and my father was holding court. I was home from college, and he wanted to test me about what I had learned. Kim was still in high school. We had just finished dinner. My mother was in the kitchen, taking the pie out of the oven. Kim was acting bored, moving the salt and pepper shakers around on the table like chess men.

'You see,' my father said, 'when we think, our minds are speaking to us in a language. This is what allows us to reason, to form new ideas.'

He had studied philosophy when he was younger. He claimed that he had never finished his doctorate because an academic's salary wouldn't have kept his two daughters in clothes. When I began to study linguistics and psychology and talked about applying to graduate school, he looked at me with a novel kind of interest, as if I had suddenly turned into a person.

'Do you mean a real language, like English?' I asked.

'A real language, or a kind of mental language that resembles a real language. The important thing is that it permits us to have original thoughts. It's what separates us from the animals.'

Kim looked up from the table, irritated.

'Don't you think animals can think?' she said.

'Animals have a certain way of dealing with the world,' said my father. 'They perceive and react. They make associations. But they don't reason. Reasoning requires a language.'

'I don't see how you can know that animals don't reason. And anyway, they can talk to each other, even if we can't understand them.'

My father spoke to her very slowly.

'An animal can only communicate a small set of messages, and the messages are always the same. A bird, for example, might have only a handful of calls, to identify itself to female birds, or to tell other birds where the food is – that sort of thing. A man, on the other hand, can communicate an infinite number of messages. I can make up a sentence that is a million words long, or a sentence that has never been said before. This reflects the way I think: I can take a finite set of concepts and generate an infinite number of thoughts, in the same way that I can take a finite set of words and generate an infinite number of sentences. This allows me to think of new and different things, in a way that an animal can't.'

'That's baloney,' said Kim. 'Dogs can think of new things. Remember when we got the latch on the kitchen door, and Shadey figured out how to get it open in, like, ten minutes? She's smart. She doesn't need to speak English to be smart.'

'Unlatching a door is not the same thing as having a novel thought,' said my father. His voice was tense. 'Skinner could teach a pigeon to play ping-pong, for God's sake. Sometimes I don't think there's any point in trying to talk to you at all, if this is the kind of argument you come up with.'

My mother came in with the pie. The warm, spicy smell of cooked pumpkin filled the room.

'Your daughter thinks the dog is a genius because it can open a door,' said my father.

'Well, it *was* amazing, how quickly she learned to get it open,' said my mother, setting the pie down in front of my father and wiping her hands on her thighs.

My father snorted.

'Oh, yes, now I remember where she gets it,' he said. 'Two fools in a pod.'

My mother looked at him quickly.

'The pie is beautiful, Mom,' said Kim harshly, glaring at my father. 'Thank you.'

He stared at her and set his jaw.

'I don't know what you're playing at,' he said.

'I don't want you to argue,' said my mother. Her eyes looked small. She went back into the kitchen. My father breathed heavily through his nose.

'Dad,' I said. 'Kim's just trying to understand.'

Kim shot me a vicious look.

'No, listen,' I said to her. 'Sometimes, when you're sitting and trying to figure something out, you can hear yourself talking in your head, can't you? It's like you can hear your own thoughts, and they come out in words.'

'Yes, yes,' said my father. 'Sometimes we are even aware of it as it happens.'

He nodded at me approvingly. I could see Kim out of the corner of my eye. I felt a twinge in my chest.

'If my thoughts come out in words,' said Kim, 'then why can't I just sit down and write a term paper from whatever comes into my head? I mean, why is it *so hard* for me just to write down what I mean, if I'm already thinking in a language anyway?'

My father looked at her for a long time. She looked back at him. None of us said anything.

Associations

A hard smile distorted his mouth. He began to laugh. The sound was hollow and joyless.

'So now you are using your own poor grades as a defence,' he said. 'For once, your lack of ability is good for something.'

Kim blinked. She sat still for a moment as he picked up the serving knife and began to cut the pie into sections. He chuckled to himself. Steam rose from the belly of the pie, releasing more of the gingery smell.

I watched Kim as her eyes filled with tears. My father did not look at her. He began to lift the slices of pie out of the dish with the knife and place them onto plates. My mother still had not returned from the kitchen. He put a plate in front of me, and another in front of Kim, without meeting her eyes. Kim stood up, pushing her chair back. The tears spilled onto her face. She drew in a gasp, as if she were preparing to speak, and looked at my father, who sat down and spread his napkin on his lap. He began to eat the pie. Kim's voice escaped from her throat in an ugly, desolate cry. She slapped her hands over her mouth, and ran out of the dining room and up the stairs. The windows rattled as she slammed the door to her room.

I sat and watched him. He ate calmly, tasting each bite, taking sips of water in between. His face was relaxed. I tried to make sense of the stillness that Kim's absence had left behind and allow my thoughts to catch up. I imagined our house as if I were standing above it, and could open it up like a doll's house and look inside. I saw my mother on her own in the kitchen, my sister lying face down on her bed, my father at the dining room table, and me, beside him. I wanted to stand up and leave him, to go to my mother, or to Kim, but my body refused to move. I was alone with him. The piece of pie he had cut for me lay cooling on the plate.

I cleared my throat.

'You know, Dad,' I said. 'Maybe there isn't such a separation between people and animals. If you can make enough associations, maybe you start to generalize to new things. Maybe the difference is in degree, rather than kind.'

My father chewed on his pie and smiled absently. I understood that the conversation was over.

'If you say so,' he said.

One of the nurses woke me and told me I could see my father. My sleep had been shallow, and I could taste the inside of my mouth. I followed the nurse through an endless hallway of doors. Each door was open, revealing pairs of beds and the outlines of legs and feet under thin pinkish blankets. Most of the patients were asleep, or unconscious. I avoided the eyes of the other visitors and looked down at the passing reflections of the overhead lights on the tiles under my feet. The smells were familiar: rubbing alcohol and body odour and overcooked food. I could hear machines breathing.

My father's room was like the others. The nurse showed me in and then left us alone together. I stood beside his bed looking down at him. His eyes were closed. His head was bandaged, and there was a fresh bruise along one of his arms. An IV had been attached to the other arm, the needle held in place with white cloth tape. I realized that I had never seen him asleep. He looked like a much older version of himself, darker around the eyes, mottled skin, his mouth slightly open. He was wearing a cotton hospital gown with a pale blue print, and I could see his body, the loose skin of his arms and the tufts of thin grey hair just below his neck and on the backs of his hands. His fingernails were too long, and yellowed. I didn't know whether I should sit down.

'Dad,' I said.

The sound of my voice echoed off the walls unpleasantly. I looked around, embarrassed, but the other beds in the room were empty and there was no one in the hallway. I ran a hand through my hair. I wondered how long I would have to stay before I could go home to sleep. I walked out into the corridor to look for someone who might be able to tell me, a doctor or one of the nurses, but I couldn't see anyone. My arms and hands began to shake. I looked back at my father and watched him breathe quietly, in and out. Finally, I sat down in a chair beside the window. I rested my head against the glass, waiting for the sky to change from black to grey to white.

Joanne Leonard

Joanne Leonard was born in the North-East of England in 1972. She studied philosophy and previously worked as a rare bookseller. She lives with her partner in south-east London. *Come Home* is an excerpt from her novel-in-progress.

Come Home

We walked past Mark's open door for days. He was always late, running down the stairs and out of the door, trying to catch the 8.33. Every day the same, leaving the door open and his bed unmade. We all looked in. We couldn't help it. The first glances revealed only the obvious: the half-drawn curtains, the duvet scrunched into a ball on the bed, a shirt hanging on the back of the chair. All normal. Then I noticed a pile of magazines sliding out from under the bed, socks abandoned on the floor and a plate of toast crumbs on the desk. After that, it seemed as if there was always something new. A pile of laundry heaped into one corner, topped with the sweat-stained T-shirt he'd worn that last Sunday to go running in the park. Unopened bank statements on the desk, a heap of them. A pint glass half full of water on the bedside table. Next to it, a book, half unread. A pair of tiny red binoculars stolen from a theatre on top of the short bookcase. The pillow on the bed, not straight, with creases like arrows pointing to the hollow in its middle. And then the dust. Quicker than I thought possible, it began to form a thin film over the water in the pint glass. In the mornings the sun highlighted a slice of the already greying desk. Underneath the rim of the plate I could see a clean semi-circle where the plate protected the surface. This made me pause sometimes as I was walking past. Standing on the threshold, my arm twitched with the idea of stepping across to pull the curtain one way or the other, but I didn't.

All over the house there was stuff we couldn't touch. His toothbrush and razor in the bathroom. I looked at the razor when I shaved myself, and saw the tiny, fair hairs caught between the blades. Downstairs in the hall his trainers lay next to the heap of shoes we kept there. He had prised them off with the laces done up while he propped himself up against the wall, panting and grinning. His jacket hung on the coat rack, and I had to cover it with one of mine. On the floor beside the TV there were DVDs that he'd bought that Saturday in the sale when we went into town,

Joanne Leonard

O Brother, where art thou? and *The Conversation*, still in their wrappers, still covered in stickers.

It was worse in the kitchen. His food was still in the fridge. We couldn't eat it but we didn't throw it away. There was a hunk of brie, squeezed into the cheese compartment with the soft flesh falling out from between the rind, a beer rolling on the top shelf, a cucumber beginning to brown and liquefy, spring onions still in their elastic band. We snuck our cereal out of the cupboards without disturbing the muesli, and avoided his tins of tuna. If my fingers brushed against these things when I reached in to snatch what I needed, I recoiled, as if I'd been burned.

There was so much of it, marking out his particular journeys around the house. If we moved it, it might seem as if those journeys had never happened. When any of it caught my eye I let it slide away out of sight again, just in case I'd be tempted to touch it, to think about him never touching anything again. Sooner or later, it seemed to say, sooner or later you'll have to do something about it.

Then the letter arrived. It was from the landlord, from his hideaway abroad. It had been just over two weeks and when I saw it I realised I had been waiting for it. I hadn't told him, but perhaps Ivy or Lenton had, in those first few days when telling people is the only thing that makes it real, and you'll tell everyone, anyone. More than likely it was Ivy, practical and cash-strapped, sneaking down the stairs late one night to sit on the bottom step, pull the phone from the old-fashioned telephone table onto her lap and dial the 'only in emergencies' number sellotaped onto the receiver. Yes, she might have been the one to do that, but it was me who opened the letter.

I'd come home early again. Ivy and Lenton were still at work so I had to face the silence of the house myself. As usual, when I pushed the door open, it scraped over the post on the floor, making little waves of envelopes across the mat. I gathered it all up without shutting the door and began to sort through it, dropping my bag next to the heap of shoes. Among the bills and the junk and the catalogues was an airmail envelope addressed to 'The Occupants', small and lightweight, with a curious stamp. My heart began to beat a little faster and I ripped the envelope open, tearing the letter in the process. It covered a page and a half, and was full of phrases like 'accept my condolences', 'in consideration of this terrible accident' and 'grant you two weeks grace'. I didn't read it properly, and kept turning it over and back again, just in case I had misunderstood. But I hadn't: I knew what it meant. It meant moving Mark out of the house. After all, who would share a room with a dead man? I went and sat on the bottom step of the stairs, still holding all the post in my hands, and stared out into the street. A new flatmate. I knew we had to, but we just hadn't talked about it.

I was the last new flatmate. I'd moved in at the very end of last summer, when the evenings were starting to get chilly. Walking down the leafy street looking for the address, I'd tried not to get excited. I'd been moving around ever since I got to London, six months here, a year there. In the beginning my flatmates had been friends or acquaintances from university and work, but as my friends paired off and began to set up homes of their own I was left to scour the paper and find rooms with strangers. My parents told me they were keeping a separate address book just for me, and laughed, although they didn't quite manage to keep the anxiety out of their voices. The places only seemed to get worse too, as rents went up and my salary didn't, until I found myself in a house with no living room, where a shower room was built on a larger than average landing, so that the bathroom could be converted into a bedroom as well. The guy who owned it came in at all hours of the day, and pretended to fix the kitchen cupboards, or messed around with the showerhead, but the ring of duplicate keys he kept attached to his belt made me nervous. I began to spend more and more time in the pub after work with my arsehole workmates just to stay out of there. One night I staggered home with a kebab in my hand and found that I preferred to eat out in the street next to the bins, rather than go inside. I realised I was going to have to look for somewhere new.

Meeting Mark in the pub saved me the trouble of going through the paper. I'd bumped into him as I turned away from one of Big

Pete's rabid jokes, and spilled his pint all over my shirtsleeve. I was already half drunk and couldn't tell if he was going to be one of those really aggressive City types.

'Hey, mate, I'm sorry,' I said. 'Let me get you a new pint.'

'Looks more like I should get you a new shirt,' he said, with a grin.

I looked at the mess of my sleeve. 'No, all my shirts are like this. A clean one would just look weird.'

He laughed, and said he was still sorry. Behind me Big Pete launched into one of his 'nice tits' stories.

Mark raised his eyebrows. 'I've got one of them in my office. He's over there.' He pointed to a group of suited blokes by the door. One of them was red in the face already, and telling a story while jabbing the guy in front of him in the chest with his finger.

'We should introduce them,' I said. 'With any luck they'll spontaneously combust.'

I insisted on getting him a new pint, partly because it was good to have an excuse to leave my workmates. He came with me and we stayed at the bar talking. I bought pints and he bought whisky chasers. When we realised that the company I worked for had been responsible for some of his management training days we upped to tequila. While we talked I mentioned that I was looking for a new place to live and somehow, through the glaze of that tequila, he decided he liked me enough to say that his house had a spare room going. Someone leaving, a pain in the arse to deal with, why not have a look? So I said yes, how about the weekend? And there I was, A–Z in hand, south of the river on a warm Sunday afternoon. When I reached the address I stopped on the street and gave it a good look. The house was a big Victorian semi, identical to the ones on either side, with thick steps up to the front door. The window frames could have done with a lick of paint but the idea of a landlord who never came round to fix things appealed to me. The thick blue paint on the front door was chipped through to green in a couple of places, but it still had stained glass in the panes, and a lion's head door knocker. For some reason that lion's head really cheered me up when I lifted it and rapped on the door.

Mark pulled the door open. He was shorter than I remembered and the lights in the bar had obviously made his hair look much darker than his mousey sort of blond. But it was definitely the same guy, only in long shorts and a T-shirt. He greeted me with a wild welcoming gesture of his arms. 'Hallo! Hallo! Come in! Glad you made it. You all right?'

'Fine,' I said, stepping into the hall.

Mark shut the door behind me and I looked around. The hall was wide and bright, despite the hideous red swirls of the carpet. Up the stairs I could see in through the open door to the bathroom. Ahead of me the hall swerved around the stairs and disappeared off to what I assumed was the kitchen. At the bottom of the stairs was a pile of shoes. There were trainers and work shoes, a pair of wellies, canvas pumps, tiny high-heeled red sandals and enormous flip-flops. Next to them was an odd, low telephone table, home to an old-style slimline phone from the eighties, with huge buttons and a curly wire. Mark clapped me on the shoulder.

'Come on in and meet Lenton.'

He led me through the door on the left, into the living room, which had a bay window to the front. There was a big comfortable armchair nestled into the bay, which was occupied by a man who I thought would be quite tall if he uncurled himself. Half of that impression was made by his hair, which extended vertically up from his head like a black wiry chimney. He wore neat, thick-framed glasses, which seemed to slide down his long nose every thirty seconds, and despite the weather he wore a grubby-looking green cardigan over his T-shirt. He nodded at me, while Mark announced our names.

'Nice to meet you,' I said.

'Yes,' said Lenton.

'How about some beers then?' Mark asked, and without waiting for any answers, nipped out of the room.

Lenton and I looked at each other. Unnerved by the impassive look on his face I started to talk. 'So. Lenton. Unusual name. Is it always Lenton or do people call you Len?'

'Len's fine. Never Lennie though.' He blinked at me.

'Right.' Normally I didn't find it quite so hard to think of things to say. 'Have you lived here long? It looks nice. Not that I've seen much, obviously, but it looks good so far. I mean, I've lived all over London, well, north London, but not in a house like this. The rooms are so big.' I gestured in front and behind me, through the arch to the dining room.

'Yes,' said Lenton. 'They are. Bit shabby though.'

I didn't know whether to say yes or no. He was right. The furniture had obviously been collected over the last three decades. The sofa was covered in deep green velvet, worn shiny and smooth on the arms. The coffee table had spindly splayed legs, and where it wasn't covered in magazines, it was covered in cup marks. Into the alcoves beside the chimney breast someone had built low shelving units out of stone, topped with wood that had been dyed a deep mahogany. The TV sat on one side, with a football match playing itself out silently on the screen.

'Sorry, I didn't mean to interrupt the game,' I said and stepped sideways, even though I hadn't actually been in the way. I felt awkward standing in the middle of the living room, but Lenton hadn't asked me to sit.

He shifted in his chair and then flashed me a brilliant smile that transformed his face. His teeth were bright white and straight. 'No, you didn't. I'm not watching it. Don't worry.'

'No, you couldn't interrupt Len's game. Not when he insists on following Northampton.' Mark pressed a can into my hand and chucked one at Lenton. 'As if Northampton are ever going to be on the telly.'

'That'll spray,' said Lenton and put the can on the floor next to his chair, his face back to the unreadable mask he'd started with.

I cracked the seal of the can, and wondered how these two had ended up in the same house. At that moment footsteps crashed down the stairs and a girl appeared in the doorway. I say girl because she was only five feet two but she was probably about twenty-three. Her hair was shoulder length and mousey brown but it fell in fizzy curls around her face. Her cheeks and nose were covered in very light brown freckles. She was wearing red checked pyjamas, and the top had been done up one button out of sequence. She was haphazard, but pretty. I could have looked at her for at least an hour.

'Shit,' she said.

'Good afternoon to you too,' said Mark.

'You're already here,' she said to me. 'Shit. I slept in.' And then she grinned.

'I knocked on your door,' said Mark. 'I told you he was coming.'

'I know, I know.' She smoothed down the front of her pyjamas.

'And what did I tell you?' Mark said, as he slung an arm around her shoulders to give her a squeeze. I couldn't tell if it was brotherly or possessive.

' "Don't open that second bottle", I think you said.' She slipped out from under his arm and shook my hand. 'Really nice to meet you. I'm Ivy.'

'You too. I'm John.' I squeezed her hand and she squeezed back.

Without letting go she pulled me towards the sofa, telling me to sit. Apologising for not being dressed, she perched herself on the arm next to me and took the beer can out of my hand. After giving it a sniff she made a face and gave it back. Mark dropped himself onto the other end of the sofa, and Lenton decided it was time to open his beer. Casually, Ivy leant one arm on my shoulder, as if she'd been doing it for years. I glanced across at Mark, who smiled.

'So,' she said.

'So,' I said, cricking my neck to look up at her.

'I suppose we ought to ask you some questions. See what sort of housemate you'd be. See if we want to let you in.' She gave a little grin and raised her eyebrows.

I realised that though Mark had found me and brought me here, his job was over. I was also surprised to realise how much I really wanted to live here, like this, and I'd only been in the house ten minutes.

'Ask away,' I said. 'Anything you like.'

'Okay then. Boring stuff first. Interesting stuff later.' She winked at me. 'What's your job?'

'I'm a book designer.'

'Ooh! Sounds exciting. And well paid.'

'It's not,' I sighed. 'And it's not really books either. It's brochures. Sort of.'

Mark laughed. 'His company supplies mine with management bollocks. Small world, eh?'

Ivy looked at Mark and then back at me. 'Is that true?'

'I'm afraid it is,' I said.

'What do you have to do then?'

'Well,' I said, gearing myself up for my usual explanation. 'I have to make sure all the text and the illustrations fit in the right number of pages. Basically.'

'Oh.' She sounded as disappointed as I had been when I realised how dull my job actually was.

'But you know, sometimes I get to colour in maps of Britain.'

She laughed, a bit theatrically, and nearly fell off the arm of the sofa into my lap. As she fell back she grabbed hold of my shoulder and I reached out and put my arm around her back.

'You okay?' I asked.

'Yeah. Balance not quite what it should be after last night.'

I withdrew my arm slowly. She was still smiling at me.

'Well, at least you get paid something. That's all we care about. God knows I haven't got a job I can write home about either. You got a question you want to ask, Len?' She turned to look at Lenton, who was just staring at the TV. 'Football? That's not like you.'

'Mark put it on,' Lenton said, not taking his eyes off the game.

'Well, I suppose I should check – do you like football?' she asked, turning back to me.

I was more than aware of her weight leaning on me. I had no idea what the right answer would be. 'I'll be honest. I like football if it's on,' I said. 'But I don't make an effort to watch it.'

'Bollocks,' she said.

'No, it's true,' I said, smiling.

'Really?'

Mark laughed. 'See? Not all men are the same, Ivy.'

'Yes, you are,' she said. She looked down at me again. 'I don't give a shit about the football, or whether you like it or you don't like it. Mark said you seemed all right and that's all right for me.'

I looked at Mark to say thanks and we ended up chinking cans.

'It's just, me and Len, you know,' she carried on, 'we thought it would be nice to meet you at least once. Just to make sure you're not a nutcase.'

'That's fair enough.' I sipped at my lager.

'And if you're not a nutcase, it saves us the trouble of sticking an ad up and getting a real bunch of nutters through here. So what d'you reckon, Len?'

'So far, not a nutter,' said Lenton.

I moved in three weeks later, cutting short the lease on my old room. I even got most of my deposit back, but I didn't mind about the money I'd lost. It seemed worth it to get out of there. I felt happy piling my boxes into the little rented van, and, when I'd driven them across town, Lenton helped me unload them into my new room. That night we'd ordered take-away and watched *The French Connection*, and Mark had made us all laugh with his impression of Gene Hackman.

I looked down at the landlord's letter that I was clutching in my hands. It wasn't going to work like that this time. I couldn't think about it. Not now. I stood up from the stairs, put Mark's post on the pile on the telephone table and took the landlord's letter into the kitchen, where I could leave it on the table for everyone else to read.

Maria Margaronis

Maria Margaronis is London correspondent for *The Nation*; her work has also appeared in the *Times Literary Supplement*, the *Guardian* and the *London Review of Books*. *The New Order* is an excerpt from her first novel, set in Greece during the Axis occupation and the civil war that followed.

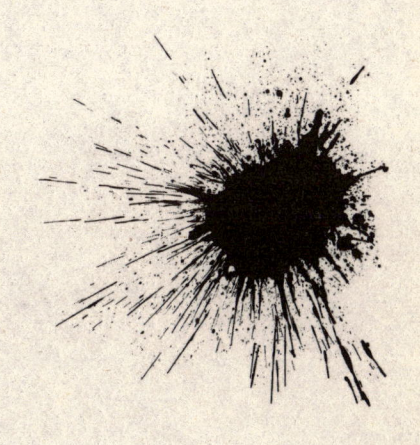

The New Order

January 1942

Roula had been dreaming of the flock. She woke with the memory of grey and brown wool, the abruptness of hooves, the trembling of the bells: small high ones for the slaughtering lambs, sweet low ones for the rams. Inside the sheepfold she could see the butcher smiling, looking at her as if he knew her mind.

Her hip bone ached where she'd been lying on her side, and her shoulder too, and she could feel the cold air pressing around the bed. Her stomach was an aching knot. She lowered her feet to the ground like an old woman and sat up slowly, trying to cheat the dizziness. Sitting on the bed she reached for her woollen stockings, her underpants and her skirt, postponing for as long as possible the moment of raising the night-dress up over her head. Once she was dressed she stood in front of the window, looking out at the thin curtains and lopsided blinds on the other side of the courtyard. The metal fire escape was strung with empty clothes lines and disordered wooden pegs. A bottle lay on its side, waiting for the wind to push it over. She watched it roll a little, and then stop.

Her room opened onto the kitchen, which still smelled of vanilla and cinnamon. Kyria Aliki was already padding about there in her flannel dressing gown with a thick cardigan on top, putting the clean bowls back into the cupboard. They had had the *emprimé* soup last night, with small dried pieces of potato and carrot floating in it and the occasional pea. When the bowls were put away Kyria Aliki started on the lamp glasses, carefully cleaning the black smudges from the chimneys with a soft white cloth. She allowed no one else to touch the glasses: that way, if one of them broke, she could only blame herself. Kyria Aliki hated darkness; each night when the power went off she sat as close as she could to the big lamp on the table, pretending to read until she considered it a respectable time to go to bed. Sometimes friends came and read aloud long past the curfew hour, from manuscripts or little magazines printed on yellow paper. In the morning Roula would find poets sleeping on the sofa cushions, their ties and shoes scattered about the floor.

'Sorry, Kyria.'

'For what, Roula?'

'I'm late.'

'No, you're not late. I got up early. Kyrios Stephanos is working already, and I couldn't sleep.'

Together they put the kitchen to rights, keeping their movements small: the cutlery in the compartments of its wooden drawer, the towels on their hooks, the saucepans in the cupboard. Roula wiped the counter out of habit although there were no crumbs and swept the dust from the floor. Then she boiled water in the kettle and made mountain tea, which they drank at the kitchen table. The warmth filled up the stomach for a while; when it was gone the knot returned, sometimes worse than before, a rasping hollowness on the edge of nausea.

Kyria Aliki put an extra teaspoon of sugar in her husband's cup and rose to take it to him in his study. 'Roula, I want you to buy bread however long it takes, and I want you to go to Antonopoulos and tell him we have to have oil today. Tell him we want eggs or at least potatoes. See if you can get some matches. Beans. Anything else you find.'

'Do you want me in the soup kitchen today, Kyria?'

'If you can, Roula. Only if you can.' She was leaving the room already, barely turning her head.

'Kyria, I need some money for the shopping.'

'Sorry, Roula. Of course.'

She put the teacup down with a porcelain clatter and took a wad of paper drachmas out of her handbag, and, from an inside pocket, one gold sovereign.

'This is for Antonopoulos, but only if he has eggs or oil. You can show it to him, but don't give it for less. Do you understand?'

'Yes, Kyria.'

'Good girl. Off you go.'

*

The New Order

Each day the hunt for food was more exhausting, more dispiriting. Last summer the streets had been a shifting market place, with stalls and carts and blankets stretched along the avenues and crowded into the squares. Trains still came from the country then, packed tight with farmers selling oil and wheat and greens. Chemists' windows displayed crates of tomatoes; stationers' shelves were stacked with bottles of wine. Those who had nothing else to sell turned their houses inside out, emptying rugs and armchairs, typewriters and candlesticks onto the dusty streets. By autumn the tide had turned. A glut of cabbages one week, piles of courgettes the next. No meat you could recognise. Olive oil was liquid gold. You had to walk further and further to scrape together a meal, chasing rumours of rice in Ai Yiannis Rentis or potatoes in Kokkinia. It was a shameful, solitary business. Only the barefoot street boys hunted in packs, hurling themselves onto Axis lorries and slitting open the sacks so that the grain and lentils danced like hailstones on the street.

In December the cold began. There had never been such a winter. Frost glinting on the pavements, the sky milky and low. Snow falling in the centre of the city. The homeless huddled over the Metro's ventilation grates, jealously guarding currents of warm air. At least in the cold the corpses didn't rot so fast. The dead were multiplying, abandoned in the streets or piled unburied in the cemeteries. Fathers died first, then mothers. The living kept them hidden so as to use their ration cards. Pits and ditches on the edges of the city quietly took them in.

Roula avoided meeting the eyes of the starving the way she used to avoid the gaze of curious men. Once she had almost tripped over a pair of legs protruding from a doorway; she looked at their owner to apologise and saw a middle-aged man leaning against the wall, his mouth working a little and his eyes half open. She thought he was raising his head to speak but instead his legs twitched briefly and he did not move again. The sudden emptiness terrified her, the way he instantly became a thing. When she got home she stared at her face for a long time in the mirror to see if it in any way resembled his. Her cheeks were thinner, and pale, and her hair had lost its shine. The likeness to her sharp-nosed father was more obvious. Otherwise she looked all right. But if she focused on a point somewhere behind her eyes she could see herself as a corpse, *koufari*, a rotten, hollow thing.

That day the queue for bread stretched round two corners and along the length of Karaiskaki Street. Sullen housewives, unshaved men, boys with their pants held up by bits of string leaned and fidgeted along the building walls. Roula took her place at the back of the line swathed in an old coat of Kyria Aliki's. Inside the coat she felt shrivelled, detached, like a snail too small for its shell. It shielded her from the cold and other people, but it was much too heavy on her shoulders. The hunger ate her from inside, emptying out her mind as well as her body, making it light so that it rushed from one thing to another without settling. Her mother's face, Anna's, Andrikos', broke into foggy parts. Always there was something she had forgotten, something just over the horizon of her thoughts.

'Don't push me, lady. I was here first. Everyone in their turn.'
'Excuse me, I didn't touch you.'
'Excuse me, but you did. Take a step back, there's a good lady.'
'Give us some help here, a gentleman's fainted.'
'A gentleman's fainted and you're quarrelling. Shame.'

Roula felt a black buzzing swell behind her eyes and crouched against the wall, letting her head drop down between her knees. When she looked up a skinny boy about Andrikos' age was pulling at her sleeve.

'Please miss, a little something for my brothers and sisters, our father died last week and now our mother is ill, please miss, God bless you,' came the whiny, sing-song voice. She stood up, shaking her head, pushing him roughly away.

After what seemed like hours she reached the front of the queue. A forest of arms, her hand among them waving a tattered note. She got a loaf of bobota, the muddy corn bake that now passed for bread, and pushed or leaned her way out of the steamy shop. She

The New Order

was exhausted; she still had to go to Antonopoulos. The sovereign was round and hard inside her purse. Each time he gave her less for it; each time he looked at her more hungrily with his pale eyes.

The tram was packed as usual, and by the time it came a cold rain had begun. There was a stifling smell of wet wool and sour breath, and an old woman pushed against her armpit muttering, 'Oh my God, oh my God, oh God . . .' She carried the loaf stuffed down inside her coat. She had tried not to eat any but her mouth had watered so much waiting for the tram that she felt she would throw up. She picked a few small, unobtrusive pieces off the end, sucking each one until there was nothing left.

The market in Athinas Street looked even worse in the rain. Tables, dressers, lamps and beds and rugs crowded along the thin strip of pavement, the reds and blues and browns of cushions and upholstery dull and confused in the wet light. An old couple leaned towards each other on a sofa as if they were in their living room, except that they each held one end of a piece of oilcloth up over their heads. Roula thought of Tepoliani, the slate roofs shining with wetness and the people huddled in their houses round the fires. She imagined her family inside, not talking, not moving, as if they were waiting for something. She thought of the others too – Papa Dimitris, Kyria Rania. Fanis. But in her mind she couldn't make them speak or move. Kyria Aliki assured her things were better in the mountains. 'It's not too late,' she would say anxiously. 'We could find someone to take you. We could find a way.' But she never made any enquiries or took the necessary steps to arrange the permits and the transport to take Roula to Thessaly.

Roula herself did nothing. Even as they were pared down the habits of the household kept her from becoming so insubstantial that she might blow away: the linen tablecloth Kyrios Stephanos insisted on at dinner, the plates warmed in the oven though there was nothing on them but bobota and beans, the glasses upside down on a clean towel to dry. She could not imagine setting out, bundled up in the back of a cart with the furniture some villager had bought in exchange for a butchered goat or a few tins of oil.

Perhaps, when she felt stronger. In the spring. Besides, it would feel like a betrayal to let Kyria Aliki wrestle against the winter alone, with no one there to help her but Kyrios Stephanos, infinitely gentle, lost inside his books.

In the remains of the food market people wandered between empty carts, stopping to peer into old burlap sacks collapsing round inadequate piles of beans. Their movements were anxious, aimless. A man in a short coat held out small bags of raisins: 'KEEP the Reaper away, KEEP the Reaper away.' Behind a wagon spread with a few dull-eyed fish a girl about Roula's age begged people to buy her flaking, dusty almonds – nourishing, delicious, the best thing for your health.

Roula wanted nothing more than to go back to the apartment, to sit in the warmth, to sleep. She paid for some beans with the paper drachmas and headed for Antonopoulos' shop behind the stalls, open only to those who had gold sovereigns to spend. As she turned the corner she almost bumped into the man with the Italian hat who had accosted her outside the jeweller's so many months ago. She was surprised to see him; he had not been to Kyria Aliki's evenings for a long time now. His long wool coat was clean, and the grey Borsalino was tipped a little rakishly towards the back of his head.

'Well, well, if it isn't the princess of Thessaly.'

Inside the restaurant there was a bustle of noise: men's tobacco-brown voices; the occasional high note of a woman's laughter. Waiters in white jackets came and went, balancing trays high up above their heads. The man – he insisted she address him by his first name, Pericles, but she called him nothing – helped her off with her coat as if she was a lady and laughed when the bobota fell out on the floor. She blushed crimson; in the fluster of passing the beans from one hand to the other she had forgotten it. He picked it up and dusted it off with his sleeve.

'You won't be needing that here,' he said, winking, and gave it to the coat girl, who wore a black dress and red lipstick and her hair

The New Order

in loose soft curls behind her neck. 'Irini, wrap this carefully for the young lady, please, and put it with her coat.' He took the bag of beans from her and handed that over too.

With the coat off she felt exposed; she put her arm across her knitted cardigan. The man propelled her towards a table in the corner with his fingertips spread out across her back. Before he let her go he flattened his palm for a moment so that she felt its warmth against her spine.

The table was set with a white cloth and silver cutlery and glasses with tall stems. She wanted to run away, but for the smells that wafted from the kitchen every time a waiter kicked open the swing door. The sharpness of egg-lemon soup, the velvet comfort of tomato sauce. The succulent richness, the brown depth of meat. The man seemed to guess her need.

'Will you have some lamb, Roula? And a little wine?'

She nodded abjectly but said, 'No, thank you, no wine.'

She did not look at him. She watched as the waiter poured pale ruby liquid into his glass. The warm light danced inside it.

'Have a sip, Roula. Don't be shy. It will give you strength.' And he nodded to the waiter, an expressionless man with slicked back silver hair, who came around to her side and tipped the bottle in its apron of white linen over her waiting glass. Its long throat made a rhythmic popping sound, rising up the musical scale.

'I shouldn't have come.'

'Why not, Roula? Why shouldn't I help you? We all have to help each other, don't we, in these difficult times?'

She didn't know what to say. She stared at the white space between the knife and fork where her plate was going to be. He lowered his voice.

'Roula, I know what you're thinking and I understand. Don't be afraid. I don't want anything but the pleasure of offering you lunch.'

When she looked up his face was kinder than she had remembered it. There were soft wrinkles around the eyes, and his dark eyebrows were salted with grey hairs. He seemed tired, sad even, with the impersonal sadness people have who have learned more than they wanted. She had seen that expression on Papa Dimitris' face at home, and on Kyrios Stephanos'. But here the voice didn't match the face. When Pericles spoke his voice was smooth and confident.

'You're wondering what this restaurant is, how I can come here, is that it?'

She shook her head hastily. He ignored the gesture and addressed her thought directly.

'Do you understand what is happening, Roula, why Athens is hungry?'

She whispered, 'The Occupation. And the English blockade. And people can't bring their crops in from the country.'

'Correct. Smart girl. The occupying armies require a lot of supplies, and there is no fuel. And the English have shut us in so nothing can be imported. And people have no work. Some people, like your mistress, help by running soup kitchens and so on. They do a lot of good. Some of us think we can help more in a different way, by helping things run more smoothly.'

The waiter returned with two plates of lamb, thick grainy pieces swimming in amber juice; a bowl piled high with roast potatoes; another full of carrots and green peas. Roula sat motionless.

'Shall I serve you some vegetables?'

Pericles spooned the little brightly coloured cubes onto her plate, and next to them the shining gold potatoes.

'People have made fortunes – fortunes – hoarding food. There are peasants who go to the café in smoking jackets, peasants with chandeliers and pianos in their barns.'

Roula still had not eaten anything. The longer she watched the food on her plate the more unreal it seemed. But the smell was filling her nostrils so that she could barely concentrate on what the man was saying, or wonder why he was telling her all this. He had tucked his napkin into his shirt collar and begun to eat, without interrupting his lecture, waving a mouthful on the end of his fork while he chewed the previous one. Somehow he managed to do this with great delicacy, so that she never saw the food inside his mouth.

The New Order

'Of course they're making the best of a bad situation. Anybody would.' He took another bite. 'We Greeks have never been able to put the common good before personal advantage. We all think we know best. We simply don't know how to work together. Roula, you're not eating. Eat, child. What are you waiting for? Do you want it to get cold?'

She picked up the heavy knife and fork and started to saw at the lamb. Her heart was beating fast. She felt sick; she wanted it and she was afraid she would throw up at the first mouthful. She took a forkful of vegetables. The buttery carrot melted in her mouth. It had the sweetness of kataifi at the pastry shop in Larisa, of warm milk from the ewe. She felt it trickle all the way down her spine. She cut a piece of meat, and her eyes filled with tears. The bright walls and chandeliers trembled around her, and a surprising sob rose like a bubble from the bottom of her chest. She caught it in her throat.

Pericles leaned across the table and put a hand on her arm.

'It's all right, Roula, don't cry, don't cry please, there's a good girl. I know what you're going through. Come on. Come on now. Stop. It's my fault. All this time I haven't asked you anything about yourself. Have you had news from home?'

She raised her eyes to see two German officers walk through the restaurant, nodding politely to the assembled diners, who went briefly quiet. They pushed open a door at the back; a swell of laughter burst out and was gone. While her attention was elsewhere her left hand raised the fork to her mouth and slipped the lamb inside. As if the mouth belonged to someone else it chewed the meat and she appraised the taste: a little dry and tough, but delicious nonetheless. When she had swallowed it her stomach curled around it like a fist. She was afraid it would come up, but she furiously cut and ate a second mouthful and a third. Then she got to her feet, almost knocking over the chair.

'Sir, thank you very much for your kindness. I'm sorry. I have to go. I have to go now.'

'Roula, wait, what's the hurry? Take my card. If you need anything – anything at all – come to me, all right? And please give my best wishes to Aliki and Stephanos. We seem to have lost touch lately, with all that's going on.'

She walked to the door without looking to either side, claimed her coat, her beans and her bobota, and stepped out into the cold. She turned into the alleyway beside the restaurant and leaned against the wall, willing the fist in her stomach to loosen without throwing up the food. The rain had stopped, and yellow light came through the clouds at a low wintry slant. There was a crowd of children scrabbling through the dustbins at the restaurant's back door, pulling out bones, half-eaten potatoes, lumps of gristle and fat. She turned her back to them. The meat inside her belly was a secret she had to protect.

She still had to take Kyria Aliki's sovereign to Antonopoulos.

Paul Maunder

Paul Maunder was born in 1974 and lives in Kent. *The War on Error* is an excerpt from his first novel.

The War on Error

'Marriage is a wonderful institution, but who wants to live in an institution?' – Groucho Marx

What a ridiculous thing to do!

A whole glass of water, he was completely bloody drenched. The woman must be nuts, thought Bernard as he crossed the car park. What excuse is there for behaviour like that? She's definitely got a problem with authority, probably with men in general. No doubt it's all rooted in those peace camps she used to go on. The police probably blasted her with water cannons, and this is her idea of revenge. Bernard slammed the door of his diminutive Peugeot and reversed recklessly out of the parking space. Well, he steamed, as he veered off toward the main road, this time she's picked the wrong Assistant County Librarian to mess with.

Within a few miles Bernard calmed down. He took the back road through Great Milton, a village pretty enough to be on one of the jigsaw puzzles he bought his mother every Christmas. With the window rolled down, and the sun filtering through the insect-splattered windscreen, patches of his shirt were already starting to dry, and he realised that Valerie's outburst was actually a blessing. It put a swift end to a nightmarish meeting and no one, not even McGregor, could deny that Bernard needed to go home early. He glanced at the digital clock. 2.17. He added an hour, the car was permanently on British Winter Time because he couldn't figure out how to change the bloody thing. It would be right again in October. His wife's car, an electric blue Subaru whose ancestor won the World Rally Championship, was always immaculate. Polished, hoovered, swept, dusted. Whenever they travelled somewhere together they always went in her car, ostensibly because it was bigger but really because she was ashamed to be seen in his 'grubby little girl's car'. They'd owned the Subaru for three years, but Bernard still felt a stranger to its leather bucket seats and striped sports seatbelts. He never attempted to put a Captain Beefheart

CD into the stereo for fear that the Subaru would spit it out in disgust.

By the time Bernard arrived in Wallingford his shirt was almost completely dry. Turning into his cul-de-sac, he paused behind a parked car to allow a school-run mum to squeeze past. He knew her, to say hello to at least, but she ignored him. There were several young families living in Barley Close. The functional sixties architecture was perfect for bringing up children, there was even a real barley field at the end of the cul-de-sac to add some bucolic charm to their memories, providing they could forget the electric fence surrounding it.

A motorbike was parked in the middle of Bernard's drive.

He pulled into the kerb and sat frowning at the machine. It had L-plates attached, and it certainly looked like the kind of machine you learn on. The tyres were barely wider than the average mountain bike. Bernard could just imagine the kind of painful nasal whine it would make. Its owner was confident enough though, having parked it slap bang in the centre of someone else's drive. Behind the motorbike the garage was closed, so Bernard couldn't see whether the Subaru was inside. Audacious burglars? he wondered. How much could they hope to get away with on that thing? He had an image of two masked men tearing down the road, the passenger balancing a television on his head.

Bernard wound up his window, grabbed his briefcase and stepped out on to the pavement. The sun brought a blush to his face. If I am being burgled, he thought, this could quite possibly be one of the worst days of my life. As he passed the motorbike he trailed a finger along its ripped leather seat. It was warm to the touch.

At the front door he hesitated. The mottled glass panels betrayed nothing. Hazel was barking within, but the sound was muffled – she'd been shut in the kitchen. Quietly Bernard selected the key from the bundle in his sweaty palm and slid it into the lock. He felt breathless, his heart thrashed in his throat. The lock turned easily – too easily, it was flimsy and needed replacing – and the door opened without a sound. Bernard crossed the threshold, put his briefcase down, and immediately saw that his intruder was not a burglar.

On the third step of the staircase lay a crumpled heap of denim, or rather the paler reverse side of denim, because all Bernard could see was the inside of his wife's jeans, evidently pushed down in some haste. The two legs resembled inverted blue meringues, or cow pats. He knew the jeans belonged to his wife because he recognised her red knickers lying twisted inside them.

No other debris lay on the stairs. The bathroom door at the top was shut. Helen's moans fell into the space above Bernard, coinciding with Hazel's barks to form a strange, torturous rhythm. It didn't sound like Helen. These sounds were comical, theatrical. Bernard stepped forward. His legs buckled but he didn't fall and, gripping the banister, he climbed over the abandoned clothes. Studying the purple carpet with forensic intensity, he ascended slowly. His mind streamed forward, headlong into a near future of bitter rows, busy silences and slammed doors. And, in the end, microwaved meals for one. Please let it stop, he prayed, not wanting to witness what he was already picturing. As he turned on to the landing he retched silently, briefly tasted prawn cocktail crisps, but kept it down. Sweat trickled into his eyebrows.

They were in the main bedroom, his and Helen's room. On the marital bed. The door was open but from this angle Bernard could see only the drawn curtains. He moved forward quickly.

The first thing he saw was a pimpled white bottom, gyrating between Helen's skyward-pointed legs. He could not see much more of Helen but the man was all too visible. A long, curving back, no less snowy than his arse, and a mop of greasy black hair which jumped and quivered as he moved. Helen moaned once more, the man grunted in reply, then finally she saw the spectator.

'Aagh fuck,' she managed, her voice still deep and tremulous.

The man turned inquisitively around while Helen clawed desperately at his chest. He jerked up, as if stung, and stumbled backwards off the bed. His glistening dick bounced gently as its owner retreated, the purple-red head nodding angrily at Bernard. Two hands swiftly covered it up.

Then slow-motion flew into fast-forward; the room filled with action. Helen lunged towards the floor, grabbing whatever piece of clothing she could, screaming, yelling oh my God get out fucking hell fucking shitting hell, while Bernard staggered blindly forward, *that* smell fizzing into his nostrils, waving his hands about but unable to produce any sound other than a lacerated gurgle. The boy – he was certainly no more than eighteen – scrabbled on the floor with one hand, the other still clutching his groin. A look of sheer terror swept through his equally spotty face as he pulled on his underpants.

'You little shit,' cried Bernard, and he stepped forward, aiming to land a punch on the boy's jaw. But as he moved his foot fell upon a lone white trainer, his ankle twisted and he plunged to the floor. As soon as he scrambled to his feet he raised his fist again, but by then it was too late. Another fist was smashing through the air towards him.

Sprawling semi-conscious against the corner of Helen's dressing table, Bernard was only dimly aware of movement around him, of muffled words, white limbs, heads disappearing into T-shirts. A pair of long black legs stepped over him.

And when the world swam back into focus, Bernard found himself alone with his wife. His left eye felt as though it had been gouged out then shoved roughly back in again. Helen was sitting on the edge of the bed, now wearing a white vest and pink pyjama bottoms, bent forward with her face in her hands. Downstairs Hazel was still barking incessantly.

The kick of the motorbike engine made Bernard jump, then came the pathetic screech of acceleration. He stared at his wife's feet, sinewy and arched up off the carpet. Her toenails were painted but, as ever, picked at and jagged. For a few moments the only sounds were their short, urgent breaths, and the awful din of the birds in the trees outside.

Her hands fell. She lifted her head and pushed back a pile of red hair. There were vivid scarlet maps on her cheeks. Her pupils were dilated, her nipples still hard.

'Fuck off, Bernard,' she said.

'Why aren't you at college?' he replied hoarsely. His face was thumping. Every time he blinked the borders of the world blurred. What he meant by this question was, seven years of marriage descends into *this*?

'That's all you can say? Jesus Christ.'

'Where's the car?'

'Where's the car? Where's the fucking car, are you right in the head? You've just found me in bed with another man and that's all you can say? Are we that far down the line? Don't you give two shits about me? Why didn't you just let us carry on then?'

'I don't know what . . .'

'Oh, I bet you've never been punched before, have you? Come on then, into the bathroom.'

He let himself be led down the landing. The bathroom's harsh light snipped at his eyes. Helen ran both taps in the basin. She reached up to open the cabinet on the wall, and their eyes met in the mirrored door. Bernard again saw the boy's dick. He retched, more violently than last time, but still nothing came up.

'I'll go and let Hazel out,' she said.

Bernard splashed cold water on to his face, wincing as his fingers brushed his left cheekbone. The water did not soften the pain, but it did bring an alarming clarity to his thoughts.

Who would get the house? Over the past few months Bernard had come to suspect that Helen hated the house as much as he did, so maybe they would just sell up then argue about whatever meagre profit was left.

He let out a strangled scream and brutally slammed his fist into the cabinet. It neither smashed nor fell off the wall. Taken aback at the quality of his DIY skills, Bernard splashed some more water on to his face. Hazel came racing up to his legs, making it quite clear that she had nothing to do with the betrayal.

Who would get Hazel? Do you have custody battles over Alsatians?

'Who is he?' Bernard shouted at Helen as she dragged herself up the stairs. 'You're fucking a boy in our bedroom. On our bed, I can't believe this.' She ignored him and went into their bedroom. He followed, grabbing her shoulder to spin her around. She flung an arm back at him, but it didn't connect.

'Oh God, Bernard, don't try to play the angry husband, we both know you're not up to it.'

She stepped up to him, her face brimming with anger. Without heels Helen was the same height as him.

'Who is he?' Bernard demanded. Hazel growled as menacingly as she could manage.

'His name's Nigel,' Helen shrugged, as if it didn't really matter.

'Nigel? What kind of name is that? And how bloody old is he? He's one of your students, isn't he? You're fucking one of your students in our bedroom.'

'And why do you think I want another man between my legs, eh? *Hazel, be quiet.* Come on, Bernard, tell me why. Because I really wanted it, and I dream about it all the time. I sit there at work thinking about fucking every single one of my students, the girls too, why do you think that is?'

'How long has this been . . .?' Bernard choked.

Helen pitched towards him, gritting her teeth, snorting. She banged her fist between her breasts. 'Tell me why I feel so fucking empty in here, tell me that.'

'Go on then,' said Bernard, 'Try it. Try to blame it on me. You know that's a load of shit. You don't want to listen to me, you don't want me to help you. You just like swallowing yourself up in self-pity.'

'Living with you is like dying very, very slowly. Every day I feel like I'm slipping into unconsciousness.'

Bernard's fingers curled, his breathing quickened. Helen glanced down to his fists and her green eyes flared excitedly.

'My life's slipping away from me,' she said.

He pulled his fist back, but uncurled it as he brought it forward, so that only his palm banged into her shoulder and sent her flying back on to the bed. She lay there, legs apart, hair showered across the blue duvet, panting.

'You coward. You can't even hit me,' she laughed.

'Would that make you feel more alive, having a man beat the shit out of you?'

She slid back on to her feet. 'At least I'd feel something. At least I'd feel half-alive. Maybe if you satisfied me, just once, just fucking once, then maybe I wouldn't have to look elsewhere. You're such a weakling, Bernard. All you do is fucking apologise. Oh sorry I didn't make you come, oh sorry about dinner, oh sorry about this, sorry about fucking that. I need someone to stand up to me. Not just apologise all the time.'

'You'd rather I wasn't so polite. You'd rather we argued more, is that it?'

'I'd rather you take your head out of that Pink Floyd concept album you live in, and start opening your eyes to me, how I'm feeling, what's going on in the real world. Or one day you just might find . . . oh forget it, I need a drink.'

Left alone in the bedroom, Bernard walked numbly to the window and pulled the curtains back. The sudden light was excruciating but it did at least blow away the tangy gloom. He tied back the curtains and for one odd moment imagined them as guilty partners, hanging heavy in their complicity with their mistress. On the floor beside the bed was Helen's red and black bra, alongside it the black shirt which she wore to show the first white curves of her breasts.

He creased on to the stool at her dressing table. Dipping his head toward the mirror, he saw that his left eye was bloodshot and watery but otherwise showed no signs of the blow. Hurt like hell though. That whole side of his face throbbed. His cheekbone felt particularly raw and he detonated further pain by dabbing at it with a fluttering finger. Hazel came to his side and leant her head against his knee. He furrowed a hand into her fur. That little bastard, what a nerve, coming into another man's house, fucking his wife and then punching his lights out. Bernard stood up and gazed hatefully at the bed. He's going to pay, he decided. Perhaps he'll find the brakes on his motorbike start playing up, or a grubby little girl's car appears from nowhere and forces him into a shit-filled ditch.

Snorting and grunting with anger, Bernard stripped the sheets from the bed and dumped them in the washing basket.

The kitchen of 17 Barley Close was at the back of the house. A room with potential, the estate agent had described it, and it was still a room with potential. The formica surfaces were chipped and scored, age had turned cream to mottled beige. The similarly coloured lino was curling at the edges. On the wall above the cooker sat a yellow-brown halo of ancient grease, which no amount of scrubbing would shift. Against this depressing background Bernard and Helen's newer purchases shone uneasily: a chrome kettle, silvery toaster, multi-coloured mug rack, and a heap of tea towels from mid-ranking Mediterranean holiday resorts.

Helen stood at the sink, shot glass in one hand, bottle of vodka in the other. She was looking out at Hazel, who had lost interest in her owner's problems and was now engaged in one of her favourite habits – tasting the wide variety of weeds in their overgrown garden. But Bernard guessed she wasn't really seeing the dog. Just as Bernard was looking at his wife, but seeing only a pimpled white bottom. She turned to him as he entered the room, he noted the tears issuing at regular intervals and the frightened twisted movements of her mouth. He thought, why is it never me in that position? How does she manage to have the monopoly on fear and guilt? And what would life be like without these miserable kitchen confrontations? Here Bernard's imagination failed him. He suddenly felt utterly exhausted.

'I'm not sorry, Bernard,' Helen said, her voice shaking.

He said nothing, wanting her to go on, to explain, plead, beg.

Seeing this, she stumbled into another sentence. 'I couldn't . . . I couldn't help myself. I couldn't stop it, couldn't say no, it all happened so quickly. I'm a bitch to you, you'd be better off without me.'

'You said it,' said Bernard. Ignoring the offer of the vodka bottle, he relieved the fridge of a can of Stella. The liquid frosted his tongue. He raised the can to his lips again, but then thought better of it, and instead poured the remaining lager into a glass from the washing-up rack. Just a flicker of a frown crossed Helen's face. Bernard never drank beer from a glass, not at home anyway, but evidently she didn't think it a suitable tangent for this particular conversation.

'What's wrong with you?' he said finally. 'Why can't you just live normally? Without all this . . . shit. Why can't you just be happy living a quiet life like everyone else. Without creating all these dramas.'

'Jesus Christ, Bernard, we've been married seven years and you ask me stupid questions like that? Don't you even know me a little bit? It's something in me, I can't get rid of it, I can't change who I am.'

'God, I was an idiot. I should have known it would be like this, but I thought I could manage it,' he said.

'You thought you could control me, you mean.'

'I should never have . . .' But he stopped short of saying it.

She said it for him. 'You should never have married me. Then you could have had your quiet life, maybe a quiet girl to cook your dinner, someone you know you won't find fucking a teenager.'

Bernard slapped the glass down and stepped nearer to her. She shook but didn't move back. The tears had stopped, but her eyelashes still shivered. For all her hard words, Bernard knew she was scared of where this could go. Behind her, setting aflame the loose strands of her hair, the sun was dripping over the rooftops.

'I loved you,' he said.

'You and the rest of the table tennis team.'

'Helen, don't fuck around, if this is over, you've got to tell me.'

'It's not over, Bernard. I've never said it was. Only you keep saying that. I still love you. Present tense.' She shrugged and pulled a grimace-smile. 'This is a trough. No doubt we'll have them again.'

'And you think there'll be peaks, do you?'

'Well, maybe foothills,' she said.

'How can you be so flippant about your marriage?'

'Maybe because you're such a joke of a husband. Maybe that's why. Or maybe because if I thought about everything I've been through I just might go and jump in the Thames.'

'Everything you've been through, you've put yourself through. You bring it on yourself then turn round and expect sympathy. Helen, you're on self-destruct.'

'Fuck you, it's never about you, is it? It's always my problems, my pills, my fingers down my throat. Has it never occurred to you that you might be the reason behind all my problems? Does the phrase passive-aggressive mean anything to you?'

'You were fucked up before you met me,' said Bernard.

'I was really fucked up when we got married. Really at the lowest ebb. Anyway, you know that. You took advantage of the state I was in.'

Bernard's eyes glowed with rising tears. 'That's not true. I always . . . I loved you.'

'Are you going to throw that drink over me or what? That's why you poured it into the glass, isn't it? Come on, Bernard, throw it at me.'

A tear fell into the lager. The glass slid slowly through his frozen fingers, then plunged to shatter at his feet. Helen skipped back but couldn't avoid white foam creeping underneath her toes.

'Just get out, Bernard, and take that fucking dog with you.'

Jade Milton

Jade Milton graduated from Trinity College, Dublin, in 2002, since when she has been working on her novel, while moonlighting as a secretary in order to pay the bills. Prior to college, she worked as a volunteer in Namibia, teaching and writing the local newspaper; her first book is set in the Namib Desert.

This excerpt is from chapter one of her first novel *No Man's Land*.

No Man's Land

Ana pressed her forehead against the window of the small aircraft and felt the engine vibrate through her body, its low hum as fragile as the throaty whistle of a bird. Beneath the thinnest layer of cloud, the Namib Desert sprawled over the earth to the horizon, vast and beautiful. She tried to hold it in her mind, tracking the movement past her window frame of one dusty mountainous dune after another, but with each fresh attempt the focal point faded and her eye slipped down the dune's slopes or along its winding ridges or was rolled over the dips and troughs of diminishing sand waves. She shook her head, uncrossed her eyes, and looked at Lizzie, her companion for the year, bent over a sheet of writing paper.

'Who are you writing to?' she asked. Lizzie raised her elfin face and blinked.

'My parents. You want some paper to write to yours?'

London. Old, built-up, man-made London. A thousand miles away. And home. Ana shrugged. 'Nah, you're all right, I can't think of anything to say yet. Anyway,' she added, 'I'd have to write two. They're divorced.'

'Oh.' Lizzie's parents were not divorced.

She waited for Ana to reveal more, too shy to force the point, but her new friend had turned back to the window and seemed to be absorbed by the landscape once again. After a moment, Lizzie returned to her letter and the familiar world of home.

A thin airstrip appeared ahead bisecting a wide plain on the border of the Sand Sea, like a black spear thrown into the desert and aimed directly at their aircraft. Just in time, it seemed, the plane circled and descended onto the runway, buffeted by the desert winds.

The girls swung their rucksacks onto their backs, picked up their bulging suitcases and staggered out of the aircraft and into the desert. Above them the sky was cloudless, an electric blue above the glaring, yellow land. A cool wind whipped the air and flung sand against their teeth, their eyes, into their ears and between their bare toes.

Lizzie covered her face. 'Cor, bloody hell,' she said. 'Bit windy.'

Ana wrapped an arm around her head and breathed in through her nose. The air was arid, instantly drying her nostrils, and smelled faintly metallic, nothing more. For a moment, her own smell intensified: cigarettes, shampoo and the sweet, moist smell of lotion on sweating skin, before the wind whipped these scents away, leaving only the desert in her throat.

Schatzkop's airport was no more than a tarmac strip and a concrete building with a waiting room and an office, both of which looked empty. The pilot set off towards this building, turning once to give the girls a friendly wave and to point them towards a large white school bus parked downwind of the terminal. A tall, slim black man climbed out of the front cab and raised his arm as if in command. Ana looked at Lizzie and then shrugged, smiling, 'I guess this is it.'

They lowered their heads against the wind and edged towards the school bus. Just beyond the terminal wall, the wind cut out and the girls, still straining forward, stumbled into the man's arms.

'I am Abraham,' he said from on high.

Ana and Lizzie looked up at his large, deep eyes, the high bones of his face, the regal sweep of nose above delicately flaring nostrils, the whole, grand set of his features, and they could think of no adequate response.

The mask cracked and a great set of white teeth appeared.

'Call me Abe,' he said and laughed at their wide eyes.

Ana was the first to laugh, shyly at first and then breaking into a full-bellied chuckle.

'I'm Lizzie,' Lizzie said. 'And this is Ana.'

He briefly sized them up and then clapped his hands. 'So. Good. Ana and Lizzie, Principal Hacker is sending to you me. I am the janitor. I am taking to him you just now. The Principal does not like to wait.' Abe gave a descending hum. 'Oh no, not he.'

'What's he like?' Lizzie asked.

'Oh, Principal Hacker,' Abe tossed Ana's heavy backpack into the back of the bus as if it was no more than an empty crate, then threw back his shoulders and raised his face, 'is a great man. I tell you, everybody says so.

'It was 1990, we are liberated and he comes to Schatzkop.' Abe had raised his finger, like a preacher in a pulpit.

'The school,' he continued. 'It was like war. I am telling you the truth. Childrens is hitting teachers, teachers is hitting each other, parents is hitting teachers and they is hitting back. They have no discipline. Cobus Hacker, he is bringing great discipline. He does not lie down. Now we are second in all Namibia.

'And Principal Hacker, he will beat those peoples in Windhoek. Believe it. We will be number one. Then I will be number one janitor in Namibia.'

'My God,' Ana said, wondering whether or not to laugh and deciding that Abe was, at least, partly serious. 'Are you sure he wants volunteers working for him?'

'I'm terrified,' Lizzie added, although she seemed happy enough.

Abe laughed. 'Yes, yes, sure, sure. Don't you worry about old Cobus, you just do as he says, yes sir, no sir, and he'll be happy. Come on.' He patted the long front seat beside him. 'You people up here, back there is for children and you two gonna be teachers.'

Ana stopped dead, one foot on the step up into the cab.

'Teachers? Are you serious? But we don't know anything. I thought we were writing the local newspaper?'

Abe paused. 'They did not tell you?' He looked at Ana sideways and sucked his teeth, then whistled and shook his head. 'Man, you are going to find out, that is the truth. You two will write the *Wueste News*. But I will tell you a fact: you will teach. Principal Hacker does not like peoples lying about. No, no, no.'

Before turning on the engine, he paused and tilted his head, as still as the bust of some ancient philosopher, struck by a new thought.

'You know,' Abe said. 'Now we independent and don't have no black servants, I think he must get himself some white ones from your place.'

With that, the bus rumbled into life and they set off towards Schatzkop and Cobus Hacker.

A wide scrubland bordered the road, beyond which lay the dune fields, shimmering in the heat as if they might suddenly slip out of existence. Too soon, the vast, clean space of the desert gave way to a narrower view of dusty rock. As they neared town, a faint smell of rotting food touched the otherwise dry, odourless air. Abe clucked his tongue and tipped his head at the plastic bags that crawled along the ground and collected against the sides of granite hills. Full bin liners piled up in mounds, many split and rudely gaping at the new arrivals.

'My peoples are dirty,' Abe said. 'They do not respect the land.'

Ana stared at the rushing landscape and what had seemed a pile of sand and rock slowly merged into a sprawling concrete compound.

'What's that?' she asked.

'That is the jail,' Abe said and then pointed ahead. 'And there is Schatzkop.'

A line of squat buildings marked the outer edge of Schatzkop, mostly windowless walls, like battlements turned against the desert enemy. As the road descended towards the centre of town, tall wooden buildings, with peaked tile roofs, like doll's houses, began to replace the walls of solid concrete.

'Is this Schatzkop Old Town?' Lizzie asked. Abe nodded absently. She turned to Ana: 'I think this is the old German part.'

In Windhoek, Ana had felt like a small, startlingly white creature walking through a city of statuesque, brilliantly and inventively clad, black people. Schatzkop seemed to be another world. Bodies sloped at undignified angles, either inching slowly forward into the wind, leaning back against its thrust, or veering to the side as they tried to enter an unhelpfully vertical doorway. A second, dusty skin covered everything. Once bright clothes were bleached pale by the sun and the people inside them wind-blasted and fraying. Beneath all this, Ana could see there were distinctions: blue-black, milky-coffee and snow-white skins, short and tall, fat and thin, frail and brawny, but they all seemed of a kind; an isolated town of strange, off-centre sand-people.

Abe turned up a hill and came to a halt outside a tall, rectangular house, the last on the street before the slope became too steep to build on. He switched off the engine and turned to face the girls. They smiled back. He lifted an eyebrow.

'Well,' he said. 'Are you going to get out or are you going to live in this here bus all year?'

'Here?' Ana asked incredulously. 'We're going to live here?'

'Yes, miss,' he said, smiling.

'How do we get in, I mean, where's the front door?'

Abe rubbed his chin and suppressed a chuckle. 'Out back,' he said.

'But it's way too big for us,' Lizzie said.

And empty, thought Ana, and then shook herself, of course it was empty if they were going to live there. And yet, there was something uninviting about the house, a rigid geometry that shut out the onlooker.

Abe laughed and snapped his fingers at the girls. 'Man, you may be white, but that don't mean you live in the boss' house. This here belongs to Principal Hacker. You people are out back, where the servants live. But, don't worry,' he added, seeing the look of alarm on the girls' faces. 'You won't be sleeping under the stars, it's nice, you got a toilet and everything. Come on,' he squinted up the driveway. 'Principal Hacker is still at school, I will let you in.'

The driveway ran in a steep straight line along the west wall of the main house, precisely enclosed by a stone wall, beside which the land dropped sharply. On the east flank, beside the garage, stood another, almost perpendicular, granite face. Around the back, and on the far side of an incongruously green and well-tended garden, stood a one-storey building.

Abe pulled out a large ring of jangling keys and carefully selected the correct one.

'Here,' he said, opening the door. 'I will let you in, but then I am going back to school. I have duties. I am telling Principal Hacker that you are here.'

He put their suitcases inside the door, but didn't enter, already respectful, it seemed, of the girls' space. Ana and Lizzie thanked him and he raised a cheerful palm in return.

'No problem,' he grinned. 'Anything you need, misses, you just call ole Abe and I'll come a runnin'.' He swept an imaginary hat from his head and backed away, pausing only at the roadside to look left and right before swinging up into the bus.

'Well?' Lizzie said.

'Yes,' Ana breathed. 'Let's go in.'

They both turned into the doorway at the same time, paused, and then burst through together in peals of laughter.

The front door opened directly onto one of two large, square rooms, whitewashed, with high ceilings and pale green linoleum floors. Each had a tall window that fronted the garden, veiled by net curtains. The second room, slightly the smaller of the two, had a further window to the side. Ana leant against the frame and looked past the houses, past the boats gently bobbing in the harbour, past the headland and out to the flat, unbroken stretch of the blue-black Atlantic.

Only a week ago, she had been sitting on a stool, as her mother lay back in the bath, a flannel spread over her chest which, every so often, she would dunk in the steaming water to reheat. Katherine had been smiling, chatting brightly, but it had been a sad time, coloured with Ana's leaving. Her mother's cheerful words had gradually rattled to a stop and they had stayed like that for a long while, in silence but not silent, and Ana had both felt her mother's loss and wanted to escape it.

Ana now swept her eyes along the vast, empty ocean horizon and turned back into the bare room, happy to be without restraint. A thin layer of sand covered the floor and piled into mini-dunes in each corner. She ran her finger along the top of a chest of drawers and left a clear white line in the pale dust. On impulse, she wrote ANASTASIA in bold letters and then quickly ran her sleeve across her name.

'Tea,' Lizzie cried from the kitchen, having miraculously found a couple of old tea bags.

'Bloody Northerner,' Ana said, smiling. 'All you think about is tea.'

A tall narrow bookcase nestled in one corner of the room, crammed with fat Penguin Classics, left by previous volunteers: *War and Peace*, *Anna Karenina*, *Crime and Punishment*, *The Inferno*, all the Brontës.

'Jesus.' Ana scanned the titles and the corners of her mouth tilted up; books had always been part of her landscape and their familiar presence gave her a small sense of belonging.

'D'you mind if I take this room?' she asked Lizzie.

'Sure,' her friend said, holding out a cup of steaming black tea.

'It's got books,' Ana added by way of explanation.

'Bloody Southerner,' Lizzie laughed. 'All you think about is words.'

They separated and began to unpack. Ana carefully removed and sorted her clothes into piles. Lizzie uploaded everything onto her bed and then wandered into the bathroom to wash the sand from her face, warbling some sort of tune as she did so. Ana unconsciously hummed along in time. When she'd finished putting everything away, she cleared a space and sat on Lizzie's bed, watching her new friend pin up numerous photographs of her friends and family and detail who was who and what was what in the Gilbert family homestead.

A sharp knock sounded at the front door. Both girls froze, suddenly aware that there was a foreign world outside of their own.

Lizzie was the first to recover.

'Coming,' she trilled and flung open the door.

Light poured into her room so that their visitor was thrown into dark relief. Ana shielded her eyes from the brightness and slowly rose from the bed, blindly holding out her hand for the stranger to take, like a child waiting to be led away.

Jak Peake

Jak Peake was born in Norfolk and currently lives in east London. Of Trinidadian and English parentage, he is working on a novel, *Rafael's Garden*, set in both Trinidad and England.

He is interested in post-colonial, picaresque and crime writing, and is influenced by such writers as V. S. Naipaul, Anita Desai, Rohinton Mistry, Flaubert and Graham Greene.

Long-listed for the Bridport Prize in 2004 for a short story *The Respectable Gathering*, which is set in Trinidad and was developed in tandem with his novel, he is planning to undertake a Creative Writing research post at Royal Holloway.

This is an excerpt from his novel *Rafael's Garden*.

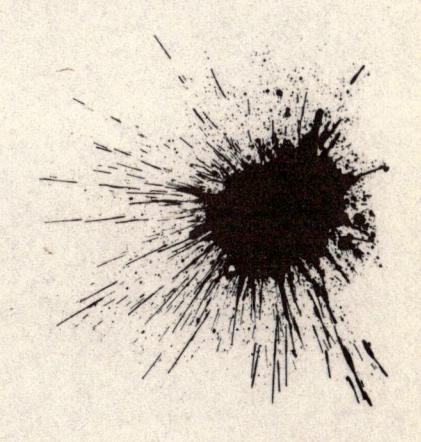

Rafael's Garden

Eight months before Rafael's birth, when his mother Mariana had complained of butterflies in her stomach, his father Imran had put it down to the symptoms of grief. Having received a letter that day from her brother Rico in Caracas telling of her father's death, it seemed the only logical explanation.

Unable to attend the funeral, Mariana languished in the house. Sitting on the bed, she cried out occasionally, staring at the walls with outstretched hands, 'Padre, padre, donde es usted?'

When Mariana vomited later that day, Imran told the neighbours that she was distraught. On the third morning of her vomiting Imran was concerned. Pacing the small house in Port of Spain he decided to ask his mother's advice.

It was already well past midday when Imran turned up at his parents' house. His mother's reception was lukewarm. Sitting in the gallery bench, she called Imran's father Doc to join them. The old man came out of the house startled and rubbing his bleary eyes as if he had just awoken from some pleasant dream to find himself plunged into a painful reality. His white lungi trailed on the floor. He took a seat beside his wife and waited for his son to speak.

Talking rapidly the words came tumbling out of Imran's mouth. 'She is sick . . . but I can't explain it.' He spoke about the letter from Mariana's brother informing of his father-in-law's death. He took pregnant pauses and stared at the orange and samaan trees outside the house. 'For days she has stayed indoors. It is as if she is afraid of the light.'

The old man retracted his head into his thick neck like a tortoise and turned to his wife. 'Perhaps,' Imran's father began contemplatively, 'perhaps she will need time –'

'It is Allah's way,' Imran's mother cut in, 'this is His judgement! I knew that He would not like the arrangement.'

Imran said, angering, 'But mother, isn't it vain to assume knowledge on behalf of the Creator?'

'I was not the one to make assumptions when I married.'

Imran tried to contain himself. 'Mother, she has converted. Even you must respect this.'

'But has she converted? A woman can easily say I am this or that – they are only words – and be nothing at all. My advice to you is this: watch her closely. I have seen her with her prayer beads. Do not Catholics also use them? If you ask me this is the work of djinns.'

Imran did not react. After a minute of listening to the surrounding buzz of insect life invisible in the long razor grass outside the house, he prepared to leave and said that he did not intend to stop. Turning to go, Imran mentioned Mariana's vomiting.

'Vomiting you say? Hmm,' his father repeated, furrowing his forehead.

'Yes, it's happened three times.'

His mother jerked forward, slapping her forehead dramatically. 'Oh . . . Pregnant!'

The next day after Mariana was sick, Imran repeated what his mother had said. It came as no surprise to her. 'I never realised there would be so much sickness. All the women back home used to act as if it was wonderful – heavenly – when a woman got pregnant,' and having dropped the smile she raised her head, 'but now I know the truth.'

Later that week she saw the doctor who told her to ensure she got plenty of rest. Imran agreed with the doctor's advice and promised to take over some of her chores around the house and do the week's shopping. But as Mariana lay on the settee, staring out at the bustle of St James, she longed for people and everyday conversation. She started to make little excursions into the street. One day she fancied some hops bread and walked to the grocers. Another day she went for fruit in the market.

One day she went downtown to look in all the shops along the Western Main Road. She bought diapers, cotton and string vests and safety pins.

Maundering into an alley, she saw a few colourful shops. She passed a barber's shop, 'Gentle Manes', and a roti shop before stopping at a brightly coloured awning. Above was a battered sign reading, 'Jins' Haberdasher's and Cloth merchants's'. She looked past a line of red and black dresses draped at the entrance and saw bolts of cloth hanging from row upon row of shelves.

'Can I help you, madam?' A young Indian man smiled at her. He had a long black beard and wore a small white topee that appeared to stay on his head against all odds.

'Yes, I'm looking for clothes for my baby.'

The man waggled his head and waved Mariana into the shop. Examining the bright colours of the materials Mariana was seized with an idea. She would sew the baby a hat.

'Sorry, madam, but if you are shopping for a material for the baby, would you not prefer a soft fabric, yes?' The man, confident, led her to a new row. 'Here are some of our finest cottons, madam. Please touch.' He stood back as she felt the softness of the different cloths on her hands. The man asked, 'Your husband will like this one, yes?'

'I don't know,' she said, pausing, 'he is also a Muslim, maybe you could advise –'

She stopped as the man scratched at his long black beard and stared at her. He replied in a dignified voice, 'Madam, I am sorry for your mistake, but I am not a Muslim, but a Sikh.'

'I'm sorry, I thought that with the skullcap –'

'Oh this,' he said, tapping the topee, 'yes, we do not always wear a turban, it is in fact because I have only recently cut my hair. I burnt it one night cooking, and in my religion it would have been unholy to keep it. That is why I had to cut it off.' He lifted his topee to reveal a neat crop of black hair a few inches long. There was something about the man that put Mariana at ease, so that by the time he suggested she buy a small green bundle of cotton, she was more than happy to do so. 'It is cheap, madam, and pleasing to the eye. Why, if I had a child, I might.'

She smiled at this and paid for the material. On leaving, the man called out, 'If you ever need to call in, please, we are always open.'

*

As the weeks passed Mariana became desperate to talk to people about the baby. Her stomach was not yet so round as to be obvious. Finding the people on her own street hard to talk to, she ventured elsewhere to spread the news.

Before long, a small celebration was organised. Mariana invited the people on the Friday afternoon and prepared some dishes. The Afghani baker Aziz, who claimed his parents' parents had travelled aboard the legendary *Fatel Rozack*, turned up with some leaven and baked bread. His two young daughters wore blue shalwar kameezes and asked Mariana many questions about what it felt like to be a mother. Ranjith the barber arrived, and offered his services – he would be honoured to give the baby its first trim. Amir the butcher appeared with a cut of lamb and offered it to Mariana. The guests ate and joked in the gallery, going back and forth to the kitchen for food.

When Imran arrived laden with shopping for the week and saw all the people in his kitchen, standing around and congratulating him on the new child, he was irritable and flustered. When he found Mariana, he pulled her to one side. 'What the hell are all these people doing here? Look, you haven't even had the baby and already you are celebrating! This is ending right now.' Imran glared at her and stormed off into the bedroom.

Giving the food away to all present, Mariana broke up the party. One girl said, 'So soon?' but was hushed quickly, handed a package of food by Mariana and sent on her way.

When the partygoers had left, Imran came into the sitting room and sat on his favourite chair. 'We have a problem,' he said, 'and I don't know how it can be remedied.'

'Remedied?'

'Yes.' He was annoyed at the repetition. 'Tell me. How do you think we can bring up a child?'

'What do you mean? You have family here . . .'

'Yes, but how will we afford to keep it, huh? Have you thought about that?'

'No but –' she struggled for the words in English, and remained silent.

Rafael's Garden

Imran taking this as victory settled back in his chair. However he was unable to leave it at that and added sarcastically, 'Or maybe you think I can dip my fingers in gold?'

'What is that?' She caught his words, anger swelling inside her. 'And who do you think would bring up the baby? Trust a man to assume that it is he who will be the only one that suffers.'

Flicking his hands against his pockets, he pulled a face. 'But the expenditure . . .'

'Damn the expenditure!' she shouted.

Imran ran into the bedroom. He returned clutching a list of bills and paperwork and threw them on the floor. 'Here, read them.'

The bills scattered across the floor. Imran bent to pick them up, and Mariana watched him. He reeled off a list. 'Electricity – twenty-five dollars – water – thirty dollars – gas – nineteen dollars – and we have not even come to the rent. One hundred and ten dollars.'

With bitter recriminations against herself for having been deaf to her brothers' and sisters' warnings against marrying an Indian and, worse still, a Muslim, she bit her lip and began to cry. Tears rolled down her cheeks, bringing a salty taste to the back of her throat. 'It is true what they say,' she wept.

'What?' Imran asked, as if he did not care what she answered.

'All you Indians ever think about is money.' Imran raised his fist in the air. Mariana screamed. 'Has it come to this? You are going to beat your own wife!' She fled out of the house.

Running off to the downtown area, Mariana wandered about the streets listlessly. She entered shops pretending she was browsing. Trailing along the main road, she came to the same alley she had been down several weeks before. She arrived at the shop and watched just out of sight as the same young Sikh man locked up. She emerged from the shadows.

'Ah,' the man said, slowly, 'Mrs . . .'

'Ramdawar.'

'Ah, Mrs Ramdawar, yes,' he laughed awkwardly, still mildly confused. 'I don't mean to be rude, but may I ask what you are doing outside my shop?'

Mariana wondered whether to speak to the stranger or not. His eyes, which were fixed on her, looked gentle; his face, callow and unlined, innocent. As if sensing her struggle, he spoke softly. 'Madam, you are clearly distraught, I can see it in your face. Please why don't you come in?' He broke off, looking up and down the street, then waved her to come inside the shop quickly. Bending beneath the metal shutter, she stood in the shadows of the shop entrance. The Sikh ducked into the shop behind her and pulled down the shutters. The light from the street dimly filtered into the room. The man glanced at her. 'You know, madam, it is very dangerous for you to be running the streets at night.'

'Yes.'

'Take me for example, what makes you think you can trust me?' As Mariana's eyes struggled to adjust, she saw him move towards the counter for something. In terror she clenched a shelf behind her, her fingers tightening.

Reappearing around the other side of the counter, the man now stood blocking the exit, his body a dark silhouette. She could not quite make out his face. She squealed as a lizard ran over her hand. Undoing the buckle, he began to tug at his belt.

'Why is it you Latinos are always so hot-headed?'

'What do you want?' she cowered.

'And another thing, what does your husband think of all your running around like a little whore?' He folded the belt in half and cracked it like a whip. 'Like a bit of Indian flesh, do you? Or is it only Muslims you like, eh?'

She stared at him, her terror lessening as she sensed some weakness in him. His grin was manic; but his dark eyes could not hold her gaze. Not taking her eyes from his, she plucked up courage. 'Where do you want to do it?'

The man blinked, his belt dangling from his wrist. 'What?'

'Where do you want to do it?'

The man flinched then wiped his mouth with the back of his hand. 'Don't try any stupidness here, lady . . . otherwise it could be worse for you.'

'I'm not trying anything stupid. Can't you see I want to?' As she spoke, a light flickered behind them. The man turned nervously, and seeing it was a streetlamp that had switched on, faced her again triumphantly. She thought better than to scream, as his hand groped her breast through her dress. He held it, and fascinated, did nothing for a moment, before tearing at her garment. Her left breast exposed, she crooked her arm to cover it but failed as he pushed her arm away. His other hand reached between her thighs and squeezed. She rasped, his rough movements making her feel nauseous.

'You like that, don't you?'

She tried to speak, but could not unclench her jaws.

'Come on, you like this, yah?' He squeezed her tighter between the legs, and began to slide off his trousers.

'Yes,' she said, forcing herself to look at him, 'oh yes.' She stroked his arm and back, and sent his trousers skidding down to his ankles.

'You are a dirty bitch, I knew it.'

She looked at his chest as he held out his erect penis. Pulling him towards her, she went for his mouth. His tongue forced its way through her lips. Opening her mouth she bit down hard on his lip and swung her knee with all her might into his groin. He howled before he fell. She stood over him. He writhed around on the shop floor doubled up in pain, cradling his genitals. 'Why, you have crippled me? How will I have children now?'

Pushing the metal shutter up, Mariana did not linger. As she ran out into the street, he shouted abuse in Hindi, 'Didi! Chod! Chod!'

She took one last glimpse and saw the man as he struggled to pull his trousers above his ankles. There were only a few people walking on the side street. Mariana rounded the street corner when the cry went up. 'Eh-eh! A flasher! Pervert!'

Mariana returned home in the early hours of the morning. Imran, having stayed up most of the night, was jumpy and nervous. Seeing her dress torn in two places – at the breast and near the hips – Imran could not bring himself to ask what had happened. He trembled touching her right shoulder.

Mariana put a finger to her lips. 'Everything is okay. Please don't worry.' Saying this she slumped onto the settee and fell asleep.

Mariana woke in the evening. Lying beneath a thin cotton sheet, she felt heavy. She was sore between her legs. Her collarbone and breast stung. Mosquitoes hummed and danced about her head. Propping herself up on her elbows she called Imran.

Imran entered downcast. He had been crying. He tried to compose himself at the edge of the bed, folding his right hand in the other to prevent it shaking.

Mariana felt temporarily pleased to see her husband so humbled. 'I want to talk to you,' she said, noticing her speech was slurred.

'Yes,' Imran said.

'You must not worry about me . . .'

'But you are my wife? How can I not?' Imran replied, baffled.

'But there is nothing wrong with me.' Imran, troubled by his wife's condition, began to prostrate himself on the floor before her. 'Please get up,' she said. 'Listen, I want to talk to you about our child.' She paused. 'I have been thinking about our expenses, and I think we can make some savings here and there. We do not have to eat so much meat – we can do as Hindus and become vegetarian most of the week. On Fridays and Saturdays I can visit the butcher and we can get off-cuts and I will make stew and soup after. Also for our clothes, I will make the clothes for the baby – I can sew and stitch them. Lastly I will need a job.'

'We will do this. I am lucky to have you returned to me safely . . . please forgive me . . . I have been so selfish.' Imran wept, his thin frame shaking violently, as he clasped her hands in his.

'Everything is okay now, please do not worry,' Mariana soothed him, repeating that she had not been harmed. Imran, still unable to speak about what had happened in explicit terms, squeezed and hugged Mariana as if with every touch she might be lost to him for ever.

*

While Mariana grew in size, Imran decreased. His eating patterns became irregular to the point where he gave up eating an evening meal altogether. He no longer spent much time in the house, preferring to sit for hours out on the gallery porch, staring out at the goings-on of the street. Neighbours would call out to him occasionally, asking him in passing why he did not go indoors to look after his pregnant wife.

Most nights he did not answer, smiled and waved them on from the gallery, as if amused by the joke. Some nights he claimed he was communing with God, reaching Allah through silent prayer.

One day he came in early and caught Mariana in his chair. Sitting elsewhere, he tried to avoid a fuss. Mariana, however, offered him the seat. 'Please sit down.' Rafael did not budge, muttering that it was what he deserved. 'What was that?' she asked, wide eyed.

'You deserve better than this,' he spoke wearily, 'and I, nothing at all.' He walked into the bedroom without uttering another word.

Mariana entered the room and found Imran sat on the end of the bed, his jacket unbuttoned to his waist. His head was in his hands. Mariana bent towards Imran and took his hands from his face. For a few minutes he did not speak. When the words came, he spoke as if every word were a blade to cut him. 'There have been rumours that there is a pervert loose in town.' He tried to laugh but failed. 'I know that he touched you, but that he did not do the worst and I am very grateful and praise Allah that he did not. But I have one question.'

'Yes, what is it?'

'Did he kiss you?'

'Our mouths touched, yes.' Mariana stared at the floor. She could not bring herself to tell him the whole truth: that she had initiated the kiss in self-defence.

Imran sunk his head down into his chest with something like relief. He had no more questions. They sat there together enervated, Imran being the first to break the silence. 'I am sorry, I had to know, I am a jealous man.' Reaching for Mariana, he pulled her to him and kissed her.

*

When Imran came to the bed that night it was very late. As Mariana went to switch the light off she noticed the open red gashes and slits on Imran's back.

'What is this?' She extended a hand to him, touching a swollen cut.

'I have done wrong, I wanted to purge myself . . . the old monks I was told about as a boy used to – and still do I believe in some parts of the world – beat themselves with swords and knives to remind themselves of the sacrifice of Muslims across the world.'

'Imran,' she said, alarmed, 'please don't tell me you have done this . . .'

'I have done what needed to be done.'

'What rubbish!' She beat him on the chest once with a closed fist and then again harder with the other. He stared back at her untroubled, as if this too were a meting out of divine justice.

'But no! You stupid man! Why did you do this? Don't you ever do it again!' She struck him again and again, each hit weaker than the last. Imran remained silent, his chest warm and sweaty from her fists.

S. G. Perry

S. G. Perry was born in Essex in 1979, studied English Literature at Anglia Ruskin University, and now lives in London. She is writing a collection of short stories and a novel entitled *The Guest*.

Seraph

A short story

Waking early on hearing a fox at her gate, the late Martha Day put on her dressing gown, and went downstairs to make tea. She passed an angel on the landing: it had been there since last Tuesday, and looked as though it were tired.

She knew her way so well there was no need to turn on the lights, which in any case had such grimed shades, and such dim bulbs, they'd have been little use. Making her way to a table occupied by half a dozen young cherubs, one of whom had lost a wing, she heard the bark of the fox fade as it moved on to other gardens. She pushed aside a cherub to make room for the kettle, which she'd set on the stove to boil.

Pouring her tea, Martha saw that the sun had begun to rise. She planned to make her way to Mare Street, as she did every fortnight, and was grateful that it seemed unlikely to rain: for months she had examined the effect of rain on birds' wings, and concluded that angels were most likely to be seen when it was dry.

She turned to a photograph hung beside her, flanked by a severe pair of seraphim, and showing a gentle-faced man with untidy hair.

'Good morning, Father,' she said. 'I hope you're sleeping well. The barometer shows no change, and there's no sign of rain. I'll be leaving soon.'

She rose to wipe a little of the dust from the glass that covered him, and after a while said quietly, 'I do think, you know, that you were right.'

Having spent his life in such an extremity of rationalism that he once attempted to find the mathematical formula for a sense of melancholy, her father had gone out one morning and found a French bible on the doorstep. Seeing it was still there when he returned home, he took it inside, abandoning for a moment his principles against having such books in the house. It remained unread for weeks, until one day, when it was raining and he was bored, he decided to use it to teach himself French.

After six months he found himself proficient, though he spoke with a strange and beautiful formality. Martha, coming home one afternoon, was surprised to find herself greeted with a discomfiting pair of Gallic kisses; but this was nothing compared to her astonishment on later discovering that her father – who'd carried his unbelief above him like a banner – had developed an unshakeable faith in the existence of angels.

'I hasten to add, Martha,' he said, opening a dusty tin of biscuits, 'that I maintain my objections to the vast majority of what is contained in this book.' He prodded the bible scornfully. 'I cannot ally myself to such sensationalist nonsense, such manifest departures from the credible! As you know, I cherish reason above all things, and it is in this that the angelic realm seems to me to embody all that I have sought.'

He poured her a cup of tea. 'I have for some years been troubled by little mysteries, such as the fact that when one looks at the Pleiades, one can never see all seven stars at the same time: one star is always in darkness. You have observed this yourself, of course.'

'Of course,' said Martha.

'Other things,' he went on, gesturing with his biscuit, 'have puzzled me. Your mother, for example, would frequently come in from the garden, thinking that I had called her, when often I had hardly drawn breath. Is it not possible that there are beings, acting fully in accordance with fundamental laws, whose actions may offer explanations for all these things?'

'But wouldn't we see them, then, if they're so often at work?' asked Martha.

Her father frowned. 'You cannot expect me to provide you with detailed explanations at this early stage,' he said. 'I intend to investigate further at the earliest opportunity, and handed in my notice this morning. I will need to take lodgers: have you a copy of the *Gazette*? I shall place a notice.'

Six weeks later, Peter Day retired to the top two floors of his house, taking with him the thirty-seven angels he'd accumulated during that time in the name of research. A couple with an extraordinarily ugly child moved into the lower floors of the house, and sustained him with irregular payments of rent. Martha was sorry to abandon her childhood room, but carried her books upstairs without complaint: before long, she told herself, drawing a fireplace in the margin of her notebook, she would find a home of her own.

Her father left his rooms less and less, though once he was gone for two days, and she found him in the cemetery at Abney Park. He sat at the feet of an angel cut in stone, which held three dying roses, and turned its face away in sorrow or anger. He'd wanted to take its measurements, he told her, but the light had faded too quickly. In time, the rooms flocked with cherubim and seraphim, graceful and baleful by turns, with wings of goosefeather and swansdown, carved from wood or moulded in plastic. They settled in pale drifts on worn chairs and pitted tables, and flew against the walls, and their limbs seemed at once immobile and likely at any moment to lift in weak gestures.

'Do not be deceived, Martha,' he said one day, as she moved aside a broken wing to put down a book. 'It is unlikely that these bear any resemblance to the angels I am looking for. Think of them rather as emblems, or symbols, if you like. Just as we must understand the movement of light both as a wave and as a particle, knowing that in truth it may not be either, we must understand the movement of angels in what terms we can. It is likely that they are neither male nor female; neither beautiful nor foul in appearance; and capable of neither malice nor kindness. We are compassed about with a great cloud of witnesses: but what form these witnesses take I have yet fully to discover.'

In time, those who had known him before spoke of him while he lived as the late Peter Day, thinking he'd begun his decline.

Martha tried to reconcile this new man with the one who had been her father, and could not: it was as hopeless as pressing a pear-half to an apple-half, and expecting to make a single fruit. In time she accepted his obsession, seeing she'd never known him so happy, and that he could not, in truth, be accused of feeble-mindedness. In fact, his mind sharpened, and became inquisitive, and he set up a small laboratory in the kitchen.

'Energy,' he said to Martha, refusing the food she brought him, 'is merely the potential for causing change. In that sense, I believe angels to be constructed, if you like, from energy, that has taken on some indefinably solid state. Now, as you know, even the smallest expenditure of energy generates heat, and it therefore seems to me to be the case that if I can make a thermometer sensitive to the most infinitesimal changes in temperature, I shall be making progress.'

Ignoring his daughter's protests that he could very well buy such instruments from the chemist's on the Lower Clapton Road, he procured from somewhere seven fluid ounces of mercury sealed in a coffee jar. Months of frustration followed, as he struggled to find a means of making sufficiently narrow channels through which the mercury could pass. Eventually, he settled on encasing in clay threads of the silk his wife had once used to mend her stockings. He fired the clay in a kiln he'd pulled up the stairs in a wheelbarrow, and found that the silk thread evaporated, leaving behind channels so fine they could hardly be seen. By then, however, his hands, never quite free from mercury stains, had begun to tremble, and his teeth to loosen in his gums; his temper became brittle, and he grew afraid of the angels' eyes, and though he could not bear to be rid of them, he turned their faces to the wall.

Seeing that her father needed her, Martha forgot to look for another place to live, and in time what friends she had made forgot her. It would have exhausted her to fight against her father's passions, or to brush away a wing or a tinsel halo every time she walked through the rooms. It was far easier to succumb to it all, and help steady his hands when he hung up a series of bells strung on wire to alert him to air moving in a slipstream, or to sit for hours drawing on thin white paper the fern-patterns of frost that appeared on the bathroom window, wondering whose fingers had traced them first.

When her father died, Martha had not yet reached sixty, and

might have still had time to extract herself from the dusty tangle of wings and white garments. But perhaps it was too terrifying to think that she had given up everything for nothing, for in time she couldn't remember who'd first opened up the doors and windows and let the angels in.

Turning away from her father's picture, she pulled aside the curtains. The sun had set alight every particle of the air, veiling the ash trees in the garden, and the spiked skyline behind. She pressed her hands to the windowsill, and leaned out, feeling as she did every morning a kind of breathless hope that of all the days past and still to come this might be the day of angels. It was no good: there might have been whole choirs of them moving through the city, but she was blinded by the brightness of the morning, and couldn't see. 'And besides,' she reminded herself, as she put on her coat, and filled its pockets with coins, 'who is to say there is anything to see?'

Outside, she walked slowly, moving her head from side to side, a habit she had taken from her father, who'd always been anxious not to miss any wing-beat or quiet breath. She loved to see the city in the morning, before it became too obscured by men and women, and knew its places by heart. She passed an old theatre decaying like a wedding-cake left uneaten. Its lower windows were curtained in steel, but once, looking up, she had seen something move swiftly upstairs. She passed the doorway of the old Roman baths, where once on its dipped stone step she'd found a feather too long and bright to be a bird's. She walked past the little wooden bridge on Clapton Pond, curving over dirty water, and tried to see if behind the weeping willows there might have been someone clothed in white.

Coming out into the Narroway, she saw she was too early. One or two men were bracing their shoulders against their shops' steel shutters, but she would have to wait a while. Her ankles ached, and her coat was so full of coins that it pulled at her shoulders and made her weary. She looked around for a place to rest, and, there being no benches, settled on the doorstep of a bank she knew wouldn't open for hours. Someone had eaten there: she tossed away a chicken bone, and picked up from underneath her shoe a leaflet printed in red with the words *Do you know where you are going?* 'We're all going home,' she muttered crossly, having as little patience as her father with matters of faith. She folded it into a paper aeroplane, and threw it after the bone.

As she did so, she looked up into the doorway opposite her, and saw a figure in white curled underneath a peeling black poster that said VERY VERY WRONG INDEED. For a moment the blood paused in her veins, and then it surged so strongly back that she felt her face turn scarlet. She tried to stand, but her legs trembled, and she sank into the shadow of the doorway. The figure hadn't seen her: it remained curled away from her, showing its back, where two sharp blades strained the fabric of its clothes as if they might unfold at any moment. She could hardly move: here was the substance of the thing she had hoped for, and it was more terrifying than doubt. As she watched, the figure moved suddenly, and sat up, and looked at her. She couldn't tell at first whether it was male or female. Its eyes were narrowed against the morning, and pale, and its hair was black and dirty. It stretched, and she saw it was a boy, with a white shirt torn at the shoulder. He raised his hands to move his hair away from his eyes, and didn't look at her again, but took out from behind him a bright piece of blue glass, which he leant over, and scraped at with his nails.

She had imagined a moment like this for so long that after her first amazement had passed, she became at ease. She knew at once that no one else could see him: a man passed by with a tray of lemons, so close that he might have touched his shoulder, but he noticed nothing. 'He is mine,' she said to herself, feeling proud and humbled all at once. 'Well, Martha. Here it is, and here you are: up you get.'

She steadied herself against the wall, stood, and waited with folded hands. Thinking it would be hardly polite to introduce herself to an angel she waited, certain he would see her, and call her by her name. After some minutes her ankles began to throb again, and thinking that perhaps he was waiting for her to show that she'd seen him, she crossed the Narroway, and stood at his feet.

Looking down, she saw that as he scraped at the glass, the pair of blades high up on his back shifted and flexed. They made her uneasy: she couldn't bear it if he went now, before they had spoken.

Then he looked up, and his face frightened her: it was like seeing the face of a beautiful girl reflected in a broken mirror. There was no life in his eyes, which were so pale he looked blind, and there was a dark sore on his lip.

Martha moved away a little, and said, 'Who are you?'

He looked down again, and said indifferently, 'I'm Michael.'

Martha smiled – of course! – and waited for him to speak again. He was silent, and thinking that he was testing her, she said, 'You must come with me.'

He paused, put the piece of glass in his pocket, and tilted his head back. He looked at her for a long time, so impassively that she wondered if he'd heard her. Then he glanced from side to side, as though afraid of being seen, and said, 'All right.'

He followed her silently, not speaking, pausing now and then to look behind him. When they came to the house, he stood at the foot of the steps, looking up, and smiled for the first time, and it was a smile of such complete satisfaction that Martha couldn't see him through her tears.

'Is this yours?' he asked.

'It's yours now,' she said humbly, and opened the door.

When he saw the other angels, he touched some, and others he ignored. He gave no sign of despising her for them, nor did he mention them. She gave him the best room, with two long windows, thinking that he would need to see the sky, and saw without surprise that he slept instantly, and so deeply that he didn't move until the sun was rising again.

He didn't eat that day, or the next, and she became desperate, thinking that he was dying. When he woke on the third day, she knelt beside his bed, and said, 'I can't help you unless you tell me what you want. What will you eat? What can I do?'

She laid her hand on his forearm, but he snatched himself away from her and said, as though she disgusted him, 'Don't touch me – let me go.'

He got up, and pushed past her so violently that she fell back. He was gone for a day. Martha lay on his bed, fitting herself into the places he had been, and waited, knowing he would come back. When he did, she bowed her head humbly, and let him pass inside.

He stayed with her. Sometimes he sat with his dark head in his hands as if he wept, but his eyes were always dry. Sometimes he came and sat with her, silently at first, and she became afraid of him: there were days when his eyes were very bright, and he was restless, and would mock her – she was old and ugly, and smelt; no one had ever loved her, and she didn't deserve to have him with her; when she died, who would care? If she cried, he laughed, and once he struck a match on the table-top, and set alight an angel's wing. She picked it up and threw it out of the window, and burnt her hand. She took all of these things as patiently as she could, understanding that his ways were not hers.

He would eat nothing, although he drank water like a thirsty child, rubbing the back of his hand across his mouth. One morning she passed his room and heard him singing something she thought she recognised, in a voice high like a girl's, but broken in places. When he slept, she stood beside his bed and gazed down at him, feeling such a strength of love and humility that she'd have knelt beside him, if she could. Once, she put her hand on his back, and felt the hard beginnings of his wings.

She began to notice that the more precious of her father's angels – rare figures carved in ivory, or white jade – were disappearing. She knew that he had taken them, and was thankful: perhaps he couldn't bear to share her, or let her think that he was anything other than what he should have been. Besides, they seemed tawdry now, with their fair faces and bright hair: how childish she had been to think that he might have looked like this!

He began to have a habit of leaning far out of the window, bracing himself on the sill as she used to do. Often she stood in the doorway behind him, half in shade, clasping her hands underneath her chin, wondering what he looked for. At these times the blades on his back seemed sharper than ever, as if they might tear the fabric of his shirt, and she would be breathless, waiting for him to make his way. But he would always come down again, and pull the window shut and lie on the bed, and she never knew whether she couldn't bear to see him go, or couldn't bear to have him stay.

The summer ended, and she was afraid that he would become cold. She went into his room and sealed every gap in the old windowpanes with pieces of torn fabric, to keep the wind away, but it was no good: every morning she found them scattered on the floor, and the windows flung open, and Michael lying uncovered on the bed. She asked him what she should do, but as the days shortened he became more silent, and hardly lifted his head when he heard her speak.

One day, when all the leaves had gone from the ash trees, Martha came to his room, and saw he'd torn down the curtains, and opened the windows, which blew fitfully back against the walls of the house. He sat on the windowsill, looking out to the city, raising his hands to the frame above him so that a black shadow fell between the blades on his back. He heard her coming, and turned his head slowly; his hair fell over his eyes, which were brighter than she'd ever seen them. He looked at her for a long time, as though he were asking her a question. When she had no answer for him, he laid his palms beside him on the windowsill, and bowed his head, and threw himself away.

Louisa Scott

Louisa Scott was born in England in 1971 but grew up in Portugal. She now lives in London and works in music production/artist management. This is an excerpt from her novel-in-progress, *Marcy Meets Velda*, set in Gibraltar.

Marcy Meets Velda

I woke up right into a panic attack. It was a clean and vivid kind of anxiety this time and not the woolly apprehension I was used to. Still, I recognised it. It was a terror of my own being, as if the real me were a grain of substance suffocating somewhere inside the heaving person-shaped thing in my bed.

I sat there long enough to let the initial feeling pass and went to have a cold shower to kill the lingering static. I stood under the water for ages, until my flesh started to numb. Lewis had left a pile of plush green towels by the sink but they smelt factory new. Seeing my old bathrobe with the faded flowers hanging behind the door, I rubbed myself dry with that. The roughness would do me good, I thought. Scour off some dead skin.

The first thing I pulled out of my case was a crumpled sundress. I went to the hall cupboard for the iron but it wasn't where it should have been. In its place were two neat stacks, one of videos and one of CDs. *Blade. Paco de Lucia. Deep Impact.* Feeling a low flip in my stomach, I shut the cupboard door again. Well, he said he'd moved things around. What did I expect?

I put the dress on as it was. The sun would have to uncrease me because I didn't know where to find the iron and creeping through the other rooms, opening random doors and drawers, would only stir the panic again. I was being a coward, I knew, but I wasn't ready to see what else he'd changed, what traces of her (and me) had been obliterated. I had a passing notion that I'd go along the corridor, into the main part of the flat and find everything transformed. The kitchen would be somewhere else, in the corner of the living room probably, and the terrace would have become a walkway leading off to another flat where vacant, smiling strangers were waiting for me.

Even if things weren't very different at first glance, I was sure I'd find something to shake me. I'd look for a favourite mug or familiar cushion and feel my insides crumple as I realised it was nowhere to be found.

But I did wonder about my old bits of art. The photo in her room, especially. It was a black and white close-up of her face. She'd let me pull her hair back tight and take her make-up off; she'd trusted me enough for that. I sat her with her elbows on the kitchen table, chin resting on her palms and fingertips pressing into the flesh over her cheekbones. I was feeling my way along an unformed plan and the result was unexpected. The finished shot looked like two people. The hands were older than the face, darker and more wrinkled, but the brightness of her wedding ring echoed the shine of her eyes and hair.

I didn't think it was like her or particularly flattering. I was proud of it though, and thought of it in fancy terms: as a study of strength in female middle-age and as an image of the double life of Woman and Mother. She asked me to enlarge and frame it and she hung it above her bed. I never understood why. Over the years she'd given me various reasons. *It makes me feel important, Marcy, being the model for such a work of art.* Or, *I like the daily reminder that I produced such a talented daughter.* Sometimes she joked that it was a warning against vanity. And once she told me it was because the expression I'd caught betrayed her truest, most private thoughts. After that I'd go into her room and stare at it, trying to force out its secret.

Leaving the flat I passed the door to her room – Lewis's room now. It was open just a crack and I wavered a moment, curiosity weighing itself against the other thing. The other thing won.

I walked north along Queensway thinking I should have brought my sketchbook. I could have sat in a café and done some work. But that would probably attract too much attention here. Leering busybodies who thought that because they vaguely knew my cousin-twice-removed they had the right to stand at my shoulder, offering half-arsed opinions.

I was halfway to the cemetery before I realised where I was heading. I hadn't been there since the funeral and I hadn't really wanted to go then. If I could have thought of a way out of it, I would have. I definitely owed her a visit.

Marcy Meets Velda

The funeral was awful. A sweltering day and whoever was in charge crushed us all into waiting taxis, straight from the cathedral. Then we had to sit there for nearly half an hour while they loaded the hearse. Or whatever they were doing. I'm sure I almost fainted. I was wearing a borrowed skirt, one of Natalia's, and it was too heavy for the weather. On one side of me Lewis was twisting about, peering through each window in turn and trying to find the cause of the delay. On the other, Nat was leaning over me, going on about my shoes. *But why the red? It's inappropriate.* I didn't answer because I'd already explained. They were mum's favourite shoes. I'd wanted her buried in them but Nat overruled me. She was probably just irritated because she couldn't wear them herself. Her feet were too big.

Getting to the cemetery took forever. To keep the cars in convoy we had to stop every few minutes and let other traffic cross our route. It was even worse once we arrived. I got out feeling dizzy and slow. Bustled along by a mass of bodies, I was pushed right to the front by the graveside. My toes were inches from the edge and I could feel the press of the crowd behind me. Sure I was about to scream, I pushed my fist against my mouth.

I must have looked a picture of despair because my uncle Val yelled my name from somewhere a few places along. 'Por dio,' he said. 'Let the girl have some room. Chica, here.' He reached out to me, holding back the people between us with a straight, strong arm. All I knew for the rest of the service was his hand gripping mine. He didn't let go until we were back by the cars. I remember turning to him then, wanting to say something to thank him but he was already backing away. When I met his eyes, I saw they were bright with waiting tears. 'It's okay, chica. I know. Your mummy . . . I know . . .'

This time I could have taken the bus but I didn't want to be too close to other people. The streets weren't busy. Children were in school and adults at work. Grandmothers would be minding the babies at home and the tourists would be on Main Street or going up the Rock in the cable car. I walked the long route, avoiding the centre of town. As I passed Marina Bay I crossed out of the sun to walk within the fringe of shadow cast by the old sea wall.

Traffic got heavy by the big roundabout, mainly coaches from down the coast. One of them must have been from further away. It had a number plate I couldn't place. I looked up at the passengers for a clue but they were just faces behind glass. They could have been from anywhere.

I turned into Devil's Tower Road and realised I was hungry. I hadn't had anything to eat or drink since the previous afternoon. In Peralta's mini-market I bought a small bottle of water, a doughnut and an apple, and ate the doughnut walking along. It tasted of nothing but sugar and each swallow clogged my throat. I still finished it.

Crossing at the lights, I turned into the side street with the motor repair business on the corner. Two oil-spattered men were standing over the skeleton of a car. They didn't notice me pass. A scraggy orange cat was crouched in the dust up ahead. It watched me approach, its look full of sour attitude. I tried to hold its gaze but, as I got closer, I saw that half its face was a swollen hive of blood and pus. To quell a surge of nausea, I looked away.

There were more cats by the chapel, all of them ribby and dull. I quickened my pace in case they tried to approach and rub around my legs.

The entrance to the cemetery was a long wooden structure, arch-shaped and painted white. It felt cool walking through and I was tempted to sit for a moment on one of the low benches. I hadn't noticed the heat until then. The thought of the cats kept me moving. I could feel their hot eyes on my back and just wanted to be out of sight.

I knew where to go. That should have been surprising, considering how haphazard the place was. It felt natural, though. I took the path that looked right to me and went along it until I knew I had to stop.

And there it was, just another grave in a patchwork landscape of marble, sand and scrubby plants. I thought it looked quite dignified: granite dark, with none of the curves or flourishes of its flashier neighbours. The lettering on the headstone was simply carved, no gilt. *Beloved mother of . . . Live in our hearts . . .* I sat down on the other bit, the horizontal tomb-shaped slab, with a passing sense that this was disrespectful, like perching on the edge of a coffin and swinging your legs. I'd seen cemeteries in England. It didn't seem strange there to see people kneeling on the grass above the grave. Wasn't this the same? Anyway, the alternative was sitting in the dirt. No contest.

The marble was hot under my thighs. Marble was supposed to be cool and reassuring. It was corporate banks and swish hotels, not sweat, death and dust. A fly buzzed by my ear and I shook my head. My flesh felt itchy and I had to sit on my hands to avoid a scratching frenzy.

Well, I thought, I'm here. Now what? I looked around. There was no one else about, of course. Most locals would be too busy with other weekday chores. And any that weren't wouldn't be mad enough to visit their dear departed at this fierce time of day, no matter how grief-stricken.

The air around me was thick and still. I could hear the hum of speed boats coming from Eastern Beach. Over at the airport a little military plane was rolling along the runway, making ready to leave.

I felt disappointed. Maybe I'd expected some transformation to happen just by coming here. I prodded about inside, in case something had shifted and I'd missed it, but nothing felt any different. Peace, I thought, that's what I've been waiting for. Peace and insight. I almost laughed out loud at the thought. I didn't even know what peace meant.

Why did people come to cemeteries anyway? What did Lewis and Natalia get out of it? Maybe they sat here and talked about her. Or to her. For all I knew, they came because they felt obliged. Because they worried what people would say if they didn't.

I looked again at the headstone. Supposing I decided to talk to her, what would I say? *Hello, mum! Long time no see. How's tricks?* Or was I meant to ask her for a sign? For guidance in how to navigate my useless life? Would she know about those things now? Was that, maybe, death's twisted silver lining, that you get to know how to do it all properly but – woops, sorry – just too late for that knowledge to be any use. And what was I supposed to talk to? Her engraved name or the stone I was sitting on over her mortal remains?

It was all too ridiculous and I wished I'd brought a book. Confused reasons of pride meant I couldn't leave yet. For something to do, I dug in my bag and pulled out the apple and the bottle of water, both now warm. The apple felt slimy. I poured some water over it and dried it on the skirt of my dress. Biting in, I had the mismatched sensation of the solid truth being slightly off. It didn't taste right.

'Tastes like pear,' I said aloud.

'Freaky!'

Two drawn-out syllables of drawl from somewhere behind me. It took me a second to realise fully the word hadn't come from my own mouth. When I did, I jerked to my feet, turning and dropping the apple. A few yards away a girl was standing on a grave, smiling at me.

'Didn't mean to scare ya. Did you think I was a spirit or something? A voice from beyond?'

She had an American accent but I would have known she wasn't local just from the way she was dressed. I took in long pale legs in frayed denim shorts and hiking boots, a bikini top and pink plastic sunglasses edged with diamanté, the kind that might be free with a teen magazine.

'You didn't,' I said. 'You startled me. I didn't think there was anyone else around. You must have been very quiet coming over.' *Or rather, sneaking up.*

'Hey, sorry about your apple.' We both stared at it lying bitten-side up on the path. It looked accusing. I started to bend down to it but hesitated.

'I'd leave it,' she said. 'It's all dirty now. Don't worry, it'll turn to dust in a couple of days in this heat. Or maybe it'll grow an apple tree.' She pushed her hair back from her face and laughed. 'That'd be cool, wouldn't it? Life outta death. A big strong apple tree high in the sky but with its roots snaked through ribs and bones and eye sockets.'

She was smoking and she swayed a little as she spoke. A finger of ash fell on the grave where she was standing. Forcing a smile, I wondered if I could turn my back and sit down again. I waited just too long. She jumped down and walked over to me.

'Someone close?'

'My mother.'

'Oh. Sorry.' I watched her read the words and felt my face prickle into a blush. 'So recent. Must still be raw, huh?'

She turned her whole body towards me as she spoke and I was afraid that she was going to put her arm around me. Taking a step sideways, I gestured over to where she'd been standing.

'What about you? You were visiting . . . someone?'

She nodded, taking another drag of her cigarette.

'Yeah. My husband.' She looked back there, over her shoulder. 'Late husband.'

I stared at her. She seemed too young to be a widow. Too young, and too implausible, even to be a wife. My interest roused, I followed her over to the foot of her husband's grave and read the name.

'Shit! David Dias!' I said, and then covered my mouth with my hand.

'I guess you knew him, huh?' I nodded. She lowered her glasses an inch down her nose to look me in the eye. 'Hmm. I see. Tell me more.'

More? Like what? I couldn't think of anything to say and I didn't want to tell, anyway. I wanted to ask. *So you're the wife, are you? How did someone like David end up married to someone like you?*

'We were at school together for a while. In the same year.' It sounded like the beginning of a long story. 'Anyway, most people in Gib know the Dias family.'

'They do? Well, that's interesting.'

Scraps of rumour and gossip blew through my mind. David leaving and not coming back, the speculated real reasons for the marriage, the rift with his parents. News of the marriage had shocked me, news of the accident less so. Time and distance meant he'd ceased to exist in my life by then. It was only a small step from there to accepting that he'd ceased to exist altogether.

The marriage was different. I'd thought about that quite a lot for a while, trying out possible faces and shapes to fit the image of a wife good enough for David Dias. Outdoorsy equestrian bore with big teeth? Flat shoe wearer with sensible hair and a cashmere sweater knotted around her shoulders? Glamorous, vapid society girl with an entrepreneur father and a faceful of surgery? All were possible but they were stereotypes. Nothing worked well enough to make her real. To me, she'd always just been hearsay.

She still was. I couldn't take in the fact that this wan, straggly person would have appealed enough to David for him to marry her.

I realised I was gawping. The girl, woman, David's wife, looked amused, smiling in a way that threatened to trip into a laugh. I didn't like it. It felt like being teased.

'Well, I should let you get back to . . . You've obviously travelled a long way to come here.'

She caught my arm as I turned away.

'No, wait. Don't go. I have plenty of time. No plans to leave this part of the world just yet. It'd be good to hang out. Spend some time with someone who knew David. Knew him before.'

'No, really . . .'

'And I don't know anyone else here.'

'But I . . .'

I could think of no excuse that wouldn't leave me looking pathetic. *I have to be with my mother a while longer. And I don't generally 'hang out' with strangers.*

But apparently it was already settled that I'd stay.

'Silent as the grave,' she said, laughing. 'What a crock.' She looked about us, flapping her arms. 'I mean really . . . look. All that information. Silent, my ass. The dead are just a bunch of exhibitionists.' She climbed back up onto David's grave. 'See.'

Marcy Meets Velda

Turning in a slow circle, she opened up the cemetery for my inspection. 'Names, dates, ages, relationships, jobs. All those details. Then there's the flowers – how many, what kind, how often, how expensive – and the cards and the size of the stone and how clean and neat each one is compared with the next. So much information – doesn't it make your head hurt? Look!'

She pointed to a row of plain white stones close by and began reading the first. I followed along, hearing her voice more than seeing the words.

'"G. H. Austen. Able Seaman R.N. J/3356. HMS Britannia. 10th November 1918. Age 26. Peace Perfect Peace Our Future All Unknown." Look at that. They all died on the same day and they all have exactly the same message carved over their heads. Peace perfect peace. What do you suppose "J/3356" means? I'll bet it was some kind of identification. Rank or something. More information – that's all there is. Nothing but show-offy information. Wow.' She let out a slow breath and sat down cross-legged, leaning her head against David's headstone. 'Did you like him?'

It took me a second to catch up. I was still at sea in 1918 thinking of peace and the future. I stood in front of her, squinting into the sun.

'Who, David? Yes. I liked him.'

No, I thought he was a spoilt, arrogant moron with peculiar taste in women. What else did she expect me to say?

She went quiet and I waited for her to start spouting more dippy comments about death and the dead. Or, worse, personal memories about David. I didn't think I could handle her sentimental gush about the agony of losing the love of your life.

'Wanna get a beer or something?' she asked. 'I passed a place down the road that looked okay. Chico's or something, I think.'

She tilted her head to one side and sort of pouted. It was an absurd expression for a grown-up to pull but somehow she carried it off.

'Okay.'

'Great! That's so great.' She stood up as she spoke. 'We have so much to talk about. What a coincidence us meeting like this, huh? You can tell me your David stories and I can tell you mine. I'm Velda, by the way.'

She stuck her hand out and I shook it.

'Marcelle,' I said. 'Or Marcy. Most people call me Marcy.'

Velda leaned in, her face close to mine.

'They do? The fuckers.'

A. E. Watterson

A. E. Watterson was born and currently resides in Glasgow, and there read English Literature at the University. The work entitled *Next Stop America*, from which this excerpt from the first chapter, 'We are Bound for the Promised Land', has been taken, is the first in a series of three novels, collectively entitled *Atlantica*.

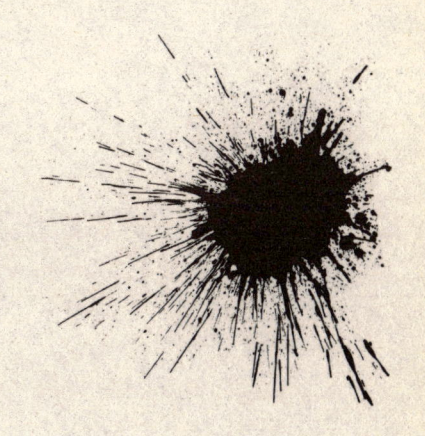

We are Bound for the Promised Land

Eilean MacLeod scooped handfuls of potato peelings from the grim, iron pail that swung on the crook of her left elbow and threw them onto the clay floor of the byre where the cow watched her through sagging black eyelids. The cow did not move, letting the chickens scuttle, feet flying from side to side and wings flapping, forwards first, knowing that there would be plenty left once their feathered stomachs were puffed out.

'Here chicky-chicky-doo,' Eilean said. She stooped to let one of the chickens eat from her hand. The triangled beak tap-tapped at the skins. She stepped forward to offer her palm to another and stood on the grubby frill of her underskirt. She fell slowly onto her knees and the pail turned upside down, emptying the rest of the skins on the sticky floor. The handle left the crook and lodged itself awkwardly aside her ribs.

'Look what you made me do, chicky,' she said. The chickens blinked their tiny eyes open and shut, and fluttered forwards to the skins. Eilean dug the heels of her hands into the floor and sat up. The floor was damp and smelt of the animals. Rich fumes made their way to her nostrils. She spread out her skirts, leaving grimy streaks on her apron. The cow lumbered slowly past her towards the food. She lowered the head that hung on her muscular neck towards the food, sending the chickens flying into the air. They collided with one another and fell in a feathery pile. The cow ignored them and continued to eat. Eilean rose and went over to her. She rubbed the cow's neck and felt her taut sinews tighten and relax as she chewed and swallowed.

'You're a good lass, so you are.' The cow ignored Eilean, so she took one of the plaits that hung over her shoulders and twirled the end in one of the beast's ears. The cow shook her head once, flicking a few skins and some hanging saliva onto Eilean. She wiped the mealy dribble with the back of her hand and rubbed it into the cow's side. 'That's what you get for ignoring me.' The black head bobbed on Eilean's front, eyes hanging on the food. 'I'll leave you

A. E. Watterson

to your dinner, then.' She picked up the empty pail and hung it on the hook by the door. She reached behind herself and undid the ties of her apron, walking towards the door as she did so. Through it, she watched her sisters by the fire. They worked over a griddle that balanced above the steady flames on an iron stand, which glowed orange at its base. Fiona flattened bannocks with the back of a wooden spoon and Mary stood behind her holding a tray. To their left sat mother, in grandfather's old upright chair. The clack-clack of the needles reached Eilean before she could see mother's fingers manipulating the dark wool. Mother's head rested against the wall, her eyes shut, as the needles delved in and out. Eilean pulled the apron over her head and folded it roughly as she walked towards the table that lay behind the fire. She flattened it between her palms and placed it on the ridged surface. Her coat hung with peaked shoulders on one of the chairs that surrounded the table. She pulled it by the collar and swung it on. As she turned to walk towards mother and the door, father appeared from the bedroom. His face glowed above the white ring at his neck.

'Eilean,' he said, 'your mother needs you to do some knitting. You and your sisters need some new stockings for the spring.'

'But Father, I've . . .'

'There are no buts about it. It needs to be done.'

'I said I would meet – '

'Oh, who? Angus Munro and Lewis Campbell? They'll manage without you tonight. I don't know why you want to play with boys. It's not as if there aren't girls your age in the village for you to play with. Katie MacInnes and her friends are lovely girls, you should try to be a bit more like them. You shouldn't be seen to be breenging in to everything. It's no good for a girl to be like that.'

'But Father, they're my friends. I don't want any other friends. I picked them, and, and they picked me!' The click-click of the knitting needles stopped and Fiona's hand held the spoon above the bannocks.

Father moved from the doorframe. The white ring settled into the denseness of his suit. He approached Eilean and she saw his beard

We are Bound for the Promised Land

move as his jaw twitched underneath. His right hand made a cracking noise as it met her cheekbone and she fell backwards. 'Eilean MacLeod, you will do as I say if you know what is good for you.'

The floor was cold and hard and her body juddered when they met. She lay where she fell, and watched father push his arms into his coat. He slipped his Bible into the inside pocket. The door opened and then he was gone. Still Eilean lay on the floor. Its coldness began to seep into her body. A hand appeared above her and she clasped it. Her mother pulled her to her feet. A cool cloth soothed the swelling on her face. 'Perhaps you should do as your father says,' she said, her eyes on the basin of water in front of her knees. Eilean looked at the horizon of sea through the small window on the opposite side of the door from the now empty chair and said nothing.

'Aye, here she comes now, Angus, look.' Eilean's eyes fell onto her boots. 'It was my father,' she began to say, but the cruel wind stole her words and threw them seawards.

'Well, it wasn't her father that kept her in, I saw him on his way up to his kirk.'

'Do you think it was her mother, Angus?'

'I don't know, she's never stopped her before. I think she didn't want to come. Maybe she's frightened. Maybe she feels sorry for the wee limpets when we pull them off the rocks. Maybe she went away home crying to her mother about it and now she's not allowed out with us again. Maybe she's only allowed out to come to school now.'

'I wasn't frightened, I was . . . I was bored! Bored! I'm bored of playing down on those stupid rocks every night! And you are all boring that want to do it!'

'Well, well,' Angus said. 'Bored, she is, Lewis, bored with us.'

'I don't think that's what she meant, she's only . . .'

'Of course that was what she meant! Why in goodness name else would she say it, Lewis?'

'She's only . . . she's not bored, are you, Eilean? Last week, with the peats, that wasn't boring, was it, Eilean?'

'No! But the beach is, and so's Angus for wanting to go there.'

'But, Eilean, old Alasdair MacInver was in a right state standing out there in the cold so you couldn't get a peat, remember? Angus, he was funny, wasn't he, with that wee bit of hair hanging over his face?'

'So, the beach's boring, then?'

'Boring!' Angus watched Eilean, and nodded gently.

'Well, I've got something that won't bore you, Eilean, and you, Lewis. It might frighten you, though, it's – '

'It won't frighten me!' Eilean shouted. She stepped towards Angus and pushed him. He did not move. She looked at Lewis.

'What about you, Lewis?' she asked. He looked at her oddly, then shook his head.

'It won't frighten me either.'

'Well,' Angus began, 'as long as it won't frighten you, you can come and play on the boring rocks again.'

'How's that . . .'

'On Sunday.' Angus gripped his upper arms with both hands.

'Sunday?' said Eilean. 'But you know my father's – '

'Well, don't come if you're scared what he'll think.'

'Angus . . .'

'What, Lewis? Don't tell me you're scared as well. Don't tell me it's just going to be me that's down the beach on Sunday. If you don't come then don't expect me to talk to you on Monday.'

'What? Why?'

'Because you're cowards, and I don't like cowards. Doesn't matter though if we're not friends, you can just be friends with each other, wee boyfriend and girlfriend.' Eilean shoved Angus again.

'Shut up! He's not my boyfriend, and I'm not a coward. I'll be there on Sunday, Angus, just you wait and see.'

'That's good, Eilean, now what about your boyfriend over there? He's not saying very much, is he?'

'He's not my – '

'I'll be there, too.'

We are Bound for the Promised Land

'Good. I'll see you after the Sunday School.' Angus smiled, picked up his peat and made his way into the schoolroom. Eilean and Lewis watched him go.

Eilean's mother held her daughter's plait between her right thumb and forefinger and picked up the ribbon that sat on her lap with the left. She manoeuvred it around the gathered hair. She leant back on her heels and looked at her daughter. She sighed. 'I could spend a whole Communion Sunday tying those bows and still they wouldn't sit right.' She pushed the left one up, pulling the hair down.

'Mother, that's sore.'

'Well, it'll have to do anyway. I don't understand it, those ribbons never stay in your hair. I think the spirits have their way with them, I really do.' Eilean screwed her face up and fastened the buttons of her coat. 'Come on now, girls, we can't be late. Your father tells me he's got quite a sermon to give.' Mother opened the door and looked to the girls. Fiona led them out, Mary behind her, head bowed, and Eilean followed, holding one of the ribbons in her hand.

'Look Mother, it fell out again.'

'Just leave you hair alone, Eilean!' Fiona grabbed the ribbon and then pulled the other one from its lonely plait.

'Mother, she's – '

'Eilean! Stop bothering Mother. Now, hurry up, we've still a bit to walk.'

The path that led to the kirk wound its way around the bay. The incline was at first gentle, then increased steeply. Eilean leant forward and dug her heels into the soft ground. The grass was patchy, flourishing only in the summer months. Fiona pulled her youngest sister's cuff. 'Get a move on!' she said. Eilean looked up and stuck her tongue out at her. She looked up and saw the coterie of crosses, blacker than normal against the white clouds that had knitted over the island. The wind skimmed off the waves and found a path to her bones. She walked faster.

A. E. Watterson

The pews were already filled with bodies when they walked through the weatherbeaten doors. There was Miss MacLeod, Eilean's teacher. She was from the other MacLeod family, at the bottom of the village. Everyone at school had thought she was Eilean's aunt or sister, someone had even said mother, until Miss MacLeod explained to the class that her family were incomers from Stornoway a century or so before her birth. She had told the class about the town. It had a whole street of shops that Miss MacLeod said was longer than the pocket of houses in Europie. Eilean had heard better since. One of Fiona's friends met a boy from Glasgow and had moved there when she married him. Fiona had read out her letter one day. Elspeth said there were streets and streets full of shops and people and cafés and cinemas. Some of the shops were even open on Sundays. Eilean closed her eyes and tried to imagine what such a place would be like.

'What on earth are you doing? Open your eyes, for goodness sake, Father's about to start.' Fiona gestured to the pulpit. Father was standing, holding his open Bible in front of him. The white pages were startling against the black of his suit. The silence grew. Eilean saw his mouth open and his chest expand. She stood up.

'*We are bound for the promised land, we're bound for the promised land.*' Father's deep, careful voice rung around the silent kirk. The congregation joined him.

'*Oh who will come and go with us? We are bound for the promised land.*'

'Mother, can I peel off the skins of my potatoes, or is it a sin?' Mary asked.

'Of course, Mary, you know it's only a sin when they're peeled before they go in the pot,' mother answered. Father laid his fork down on his plate. He brought his hands together in front of him. Mary looked at the potato she was holding. It was still wearing half of its jacket, the other half trailing on her plate. It fell, landing beside a dod of turnip. Father watched her for a moment before continuing with his food. Eilean felt the dampness in her pocket grow from the peas she had saved from her broth.

Once the meal was over, Eilean rushed into her coat and made for the door. 'Eilean!' her mother shouted.

'Not so fast, Eilean.' Fiona appeared at her side. 'I saw what you were doing with those peas. Give them to me.' Eilean delved into her pocket and threw the peas at Fiona's feet.

'Eilean, will you take this spool of thread to Mrs MacIver after? She lent me it last week for fixing Mary's skirt. She's a nice old soul, she'll probably be glad of the company. I know it's Sunday, but I'm sure your father wouldn't mind if you were a wee bit later back.' Mother held out a wooden spool, wound with thread. Eilean took it and slid it into her pocket.

We are bound for the promised land, we're bound for the promised land. Oh who will come and go with us?

Ellie Watts Russell

Ellie Watts Russell was born in 1979 and grew up in Oundle, Northamptonshire. She studied English Literature at the University of Newcastle before moving to London. In 2006 she was appointed Writer-in-Residence at HMP Ashwell. This excerpt is from chapter eight of her novel-in-progress, *The Lodge*.

The Lodge

This is the sort of pub I'd never go into back home. There are shamrocks painted gold on its dark walls and black and white photos in frames dyed to make them look old. The signs to the toilet are all in a Celtic font and above the bathroom door the remains of green and orange bunting still hang from St Patrick's day. The only Irish in here are behind the bar, except at the weekends when someone with a fiddle stands in the corner and plays. But on our joint nights off from the lodge this is where Imogen and I would hang out in the summer. A girl she met in her art class had a job clearing dirty glasses and she'd bring us free drinks when she had the chance or slip us the leftovers that had only been half finished. We made cocktails from dregs and gave them appropriate names. The Danielle, we would say, watching brown cream liqueur curdle in red wine.

In the bathroom I have to sit on the sink facing the cubicles to wash out the booze I've spilt on my clothes and then crouch under the hand dryer. I let air blow tunnels through my T-shirt, down my neck and along my spine. I shiver even though it's hot. Something sticky has seeped all the way through to my pants so I dry that too, holding out the back of my jeans. They inflate at the knees where I've stretched them. Reflected in the metal funnel of the dryer, my face distorts with the curve of the polished nozzle. It pulls my lips down at the edges and doubles the size of my nose. I'm bone white from the ultraviolet. In this part of town all the toilets are lit this way so that junkies can't find their veins. On the street corner you can buy fresh needles from a dispenser the same as a cigarette machine. The two seem like a contradiction to me. I practise a spectral smile at myself in the silver. It replays as a grimace.

John returns to our table with his hands full.

'Drinks for the ladies,' he says.

It had been his idea to go out after the Happiness Group and he's kept them coming all night. I'm not unaware of an agenda. Gin and vodka for me, liquids you can see through, and peach alcopops for Marie which she sucks up a straw pulling in her cheeks whenever she thinks John is watching. Somewhere between the meeting room and the pub she has added blusher to her cheeks in two thick thumb marks. Glitter clings to the creases round her eyes. When she blinks you can see where it has gathered in her sockets in a crystallised line, frosted spider's legs hanging on loose skin. Julia sticks to drinking soda. She says her husband Bob won't stand for the smell of alcohol on her breath.

Our conversation so far hasn't been much different from our session earlier. Marie talks about herself, Julia talks about her marriage, I talk about the lodge. The only difference is that John has stopped writing it all down. Halfway through the class I had leant over to his desk.

'Don't worry, you won't get tested,' I told him.

At the break he walked up to me and explained that it's an occupational habit.

'Being a lawyer's just about taking notes,' he said.

He smoothed down his hair while we spoke, light brown, muted from the hair gels he uses. I imagine he's one of those men who keep money in a clip. When I made myself a cup of tea John had reached across and dipped in his biscuit. He thought we were flirting.

Over the latest round of drinks Marie tries to persuade John to join the mountain retreat. Both she and Julia have made a pact to go and have formed a plan so that Bob won't suspect. Marie has to phone Julia up at home the day before so that they can pretend to talk about a mandatory teacher training camp. I stay quiet, in part because I can't focus on any particular strand of conversation, but also so that neither of them will ask if I'm going. When my head gets like this I only seem able to keep a hold on the little things, the bigger picture won't stay still, like those posters made up of dots you have to stare at to understand.

'It won't be just talking all the time,' Marie reassures John.

She touches his cuff when she speaks to him but when John answers her questions he doesn't look at her but eyeballs me. They're the same eyes as mine, no particular colour at all. An optician I once saw couldn't pin them down. From afar they're neither blue, nor brown, nor green but up close you can see that they're all three in no particular order. Sludge, I had told the optician, and he didn't disagree. Someone behind the bar dries pint glasses with a tea towel in time to the music, each rotation hits a beat. John drums his fingers on the table, wide and thick, one of his for two of mine. Every other finger drop he looks at me.

'I don't do dancing,' Julia says, 'not even if I'm really pissed.'

She stares at the students in the far corner. They weave round each other and jump up and down when a song ends. One girl grabs another girl's hand and they mimic tangoing across the small dance floor. They pretend to look stern and charge with their arms outstretched and cheeks clasped together. At the corner the taller of the two girls bends the partner right back so that she can kick her leg high into the air.

'At my wedding Bob said he'd have to dance with all four bridesmaids to make up for one of me.'

I try to imagine Julia as a bride. Even though we've been going to Happiness for six weeks she still turns pink whenever she has to talk. You can tell she's building up to say something from the way her hands shake and she has to squeeze them between her knees to keep them still. When she gets up to go to the toilet or get herself a cup of tea there's a look of concentration on her face as if she's working hard for people not to notice her. She makes sure she doesn't bang into table corners or put her mug down too noisily; every movement an apology of some sort. She must have been crazy about Bob just to survive their wedding day.

Marie lets us know that dancing is her favourite thing.

'I could go all night,' she says.

She rolls her shoulders in circles, swaying the top half of her body and tipping her head in time to the music. Today she has swapped her butterfly top for a T-shirt with a catchphrase on the front, 'Blondes Do It Better'. Where her bra is too tight an overflow of flesh underlines the printed words. She taps her feet against the bar stool. Happiness is only one of a number of groups that Marie's signed up to since her move to Oz. She has her week organised

Ellie Watts Russell

so that every day is covered. Monday is yoga and on Tuesday she goes to the gym and takes dance classes with girls from her office. Jazz Dance for Pop Videos. They practise in front of a TV, play the latest music videos and copy all the moves. At the end of the week she and the girls go out on the town. Marie calls it her dating club. They drink in the glass-fronted bars on the waterfront where a waiter will bring orders to your table and they serve a strawberry in the sparkling wine.

When John asks me to dance I don't say no.

'Let's cut some rug.'

The offer seems out of place, it's something my dad would say. I need the help of John's hand just to get off my seat.

'Is that a legal term?' I ask him.

It's as bad as dunking a biscuit in someone else's tea.

The music in the bar isn't really the kind worth dancing to but John swings me around and I let my rag doll body follow after him. He unrolls me like a lizard tongue and pulls me back in towards his chest. Marie and Julia, the students, the slot machine, the barmen; they all waltz past as if they're the ones doing the twirling. The next time I'm drawn in I cling on to John's jacket. I prop the crown of my head below his shoulder and focus on the floor. We shuffle in a circle. His polished shoes slide next to mine, hard leather with liquorish laces and needle-hole patterns on top. My tired trainers try and keep up. The last time I felt this far gone was Valentine's when Imogen and I had a steak supper at the lodge and drank wine out of a box. On the walk home she held my hair while I threw up into a hedge.

I have no intention of being sick on John so I keep my eyes on his shoes until everything else stops spinning. I let him rest his hands on my back and hook my thumbs into his waist band. My cheek tilts into his chest and where he has undone his collar my face touches a triangle of his skin. For the moment I am happy to sway and stare at John's feet and I guess he feels the same. I try hard not to pretend he is someone else. Behind us I can hear the barman clearing up my broken glass, a brush scratching along the floor and the wind-chime scatter of shards dropping into a metal bin. When they finally turn off the music and flash the pub lights to scare us out John walks me to his apartment. My head stays in his shoulder and I half close my eyes. I almost believe we're still dancing. He chaperones me away from the puddles.

John lives in one of the city boy apartments in central Sydney. Despite the needle-vending machines there are deluxe flats all round this area, tower blocks with night porters sandwiched between fried chicken shops and strip joints. There's a bar on the corner that runs Miss Backpacker competitions with a cash prize of two grand where English girls dance in bikinis and cork hats. John's flat is really just one large room with a balcony. He shows me around, sliding open the glass panels at the back. His view looks straight into a neighbour's bedroom and on the yard floor below used tea bags collect in polka-dot piles thrown from a window above. John tells me about the plunge pool on the roof.

'You can see all the way to the harbour.'

I nod and make the right noise. I move my eyebrows in a gesture of surprise and then approval. They feel detached from my face and take a long time to come down. The tea bags lie like domino holes on the tiles below. We go inside. Even though he has a laminated floor John makes me take my shoes off and points out a black scuff mark on the replica wood. His lace-ups are by the front door. Both my bare feet, sweaty from dancing, leave damp outlines as I walk to the bed. Ghost steps, a sticky trace evaporating. I peel my heels off the ground and my toes linger behind.

We make a start at something. John pulls my trousers down and I lift my hips to help. Where did Marie and Julia go? I watch him take off his shirt, one button at a time. They left without saying goodbye. He pushes me up the bed and I make a show of supplication, my body parts malleable in his hands. I'm soft wax then hard as a board, my knee bending at will then closing him out. It's role play but only one of us has noticed. He crosses my hands behind my head so I'm pinioned by his weight. My limbs perform, they know their cues, but I'm only here skin deep and while my flesh reacts everything below is still and cold and unmoveable. Except for my head which whirs on as before. Tick, tick, tick. I hear it humming when I close my eyes. He turns me on my side, I roll like driftwood. Tick, tick, tick. When I close my eyes I'm still turning, over and over again. This is good for me I think, it's therapeutic.

John sleeps on his side with his arm across my waist. He has a strong nose which arcs but without a hook, like the gradient we'd draw with a compass at school. Some people think attraction is about being blind to the detail, that we'd never fall in love if we really saw people for how they are. I disagree. I'm a sucker for the specific, the shape of an ear or the bone in a forearm, ex-boyfriends can be conjured up by a body part. I've been in love with a knee. It works the same in reverse. When Imogen was mending a bruised heart I told her to find one bad thing, a rotten apple, and the rest would follow. All it takes is a sweaty upper lip, I said, or a squinty eye. Sooner or later when you think about a person that's all you see. I lie on my back and watch the outline of John's nose bisecting the dark.

Against the wall shoes stand in a regimented line, ordered in style; work, basketball pumps, sandals for the beach. A light flicks on in the building across the way. Then off again leaving me blind. A face stares from behind the window. It hangs in the dark, dismembered and unrecognisable at first. Then I see; my eyes, my head, resting on a pillow, reflected in the glass. I am frowning at myself, disapproving of me. I didn't know I could be so judgemental. My upturned belly and the suntan outline, like a negative, where underwear should be. Suddenly I want to be curled with my knees to my chest not spread out for view. I unlock John's arm and pull the sheets to my chin. I count tea bags in my head until I fall asleep.

At five a.m. the bedside clock winks at me, the perpendicular flick of small neon lines reshaping to form each new time. I lean over and upturn the clock but green light bounces back from the white surface of the side table and into John's face. He flinches in his sleep. I wedge it down the gap between the mattress and the wall, luminous fingers of light climb the headboard. I sever them with a pillow. When I make my exit I'm walking as I did in the pub, like a thief with my shoes in my hand. I hold my breath the whole way to the door.

The street outside is as busy at this hour as it is in the day. A man in the taxi queue holds an umbrella above his head even though it's stopped raining. He pulls up his collar against a wind that isn't there, an attempt to be inconspicuous. I take off my coat as if to prove a point. In the doorway a woman bangs a can. She sits on a step with her skirt pulled up to her knees and her legs wide apart, letting a handful of change fall through her hand. When she sees me watching she shakes the tin and spits on the floor. Her skin scaled and black, burnt wood feet darker than the pavement.

When you arrive in this country, a conveyor-belt floor at the airport carries you past illuminated billboards. 'Welcome to Australia'. Painted smiling faces, men holding spears against an umbra backdrop. Imogen told me this is how it is in the middle, but in the city the aboriginals busk for money in the harbour. They play didgeridoos alongside a cassette tape and charge tourists for photos.

The woman on the step talks to herself and pulls at her hair. She throws an empty takeaway container at the ankles of the umbrella man. He crosses the road and waits on the other side. Before my taxi arrives I search out spare change in the pocket of my coat and drop a dollar in her tin. As I stoop down I can smell her hair, matted stalks, like tar. She whispers in my ear.

'Bitch.'

The whole journey home I can taste her, damp compost rotting on my tongue.

North of the city I ask the taxi driver to take me further than I need to go, past my flat and beyond the road that leads down to the lodge, all the way to the furthest end of the beach. Every so often the driver checks on me in his rear view mirror. He sees clothes stained from drink, coalhole eyes smeared with mascara. There are photos of his family pinned up on the dashboard and he says he has daughters the same age. I fumble with my wallet. Before he drives away he tells me to take care of myself. It sounds like a plea.

The sand has a pitted crust, dimpled and hardened by the rain, which splinters under my feet like thin ice. The white heads of seagulls bob in the dark. They stand in clusters on one leg and watch the last of the moon. I sit and watch too. I see the darkness lift, black to grey, and the egg yolk sun when it cracks on the horizon. For a while they hang together, the sun and the moon, and I wonder how this is possible. The gulls thaw, twisting their necks and shaking their wings. They jump when a wave comes in.

All of this and I still can't be happy. I'm not blind to the self-indulgence. I've lugged my misery halfway across the globe like a dead body. It's there now floating in the shallows, face down but smiling. It's a smile I know. Before I left home I went to visit the man I was still in love with. They let me sit on the end of the hospital bed, his wrists tied up in bandages, as if he were held together with tape. He drank orange juice through a straw. When I got up to leave he smiled at me.

'Worse things have happened at sea,' he said.

His smile lasted all the way to the door.

A jogger moves along the water line, body tilting against the rake. He crosses in front of me with his fists clenched and leaps the stairs to the esplanade two at a time. I stand, shake loose my bones and unpeel my clothes down to my T-shirt and pants. My jeans lie like a husk at my feet. Damp sand squeaks when I walk. The waves are half the size of yesterday's but when I wade into the suds they pummel my thighs and leave raw slap marks against my waist. I push further. Beyond the break the water is slower and deeper, gathering composure before the wild dash for the shore. I float on my back and let the rip carry me. A song I danced to with John loops in my head, I have to hum to let it out. I don't know the words so I sing the same tune but with stolen lyrics.

'Strange angels make this planet glow . . .'

I sing it again and again. My submerged ears hear the words from somewhere further away than my mouth.

When I look up I've been carried halfway down the beach and my discarded clothes are only a nail-sized dot in the distance. I've drifted past fishermen, the surf school, a sewage pipe, but only seen the sky. I begin to swim but the tide won't let me back. My lumbering arms beat against its pull in an attempt at front crawl. I tread water and move no further forward. When I shout my call seems quieter than a sigh. No heads turn and it's too early for a lifeguard. I bob and feel strangely resigned, as if this is how I might spend the rest of my life, a buoy at sea. It wouldn't feel much different. Someone lets a dog off a lead and it charges at the water, bowing down on its front paws and threatening the sea with barks. I feel sure the owner can see me and wave. The man calls the dog to heel and moves on.

Tick, tick, tick. The background noise of my head again, a countdown, louder than in John's flat. A flood of panic. I clasp my hands together into an arrow point and swim hard with my legs. I kick in time to the beats. A wave carries me with it and for a moment I hang on its back and I think I'm going to be sucked in reverse, but as the wave breaks I am tipped over the edge and we drop together to the floor. Down onto shingle and the shards of shell like broken sweets. When the wave retreats I am dragged a short way with it, washed up with my top round my neck and my chest exposed. And everything is quiet but the thud of my heart.

•

H. C. Whittam

Angerona is H. C. Whittam's novel-in-progress. She studied Classics at Bristol University and chose to set the novel against a backdrop of Classical Archaeology. She currently works as a call handler for the NSPCC and the dark side of childhood both in ancient and contemporary times is the theme of the novel. This excerpt is from chapter two of *Angerona*.

Angerona

Rain patters on the hood of my anorak as I follow V along the lane and through the gate. In front of us is a valley. The hills behind it are hidden by morning mist. There are trenches dug into the field and crows circle mounds of earth against the lilac sky.

'Come on,' she says over her shoulder. I trudge after her. The ground is uneven and my feet disappear into potholes. I look down at them and make my way across patches of yellow grass. The wind is tearing at my coat. We come to a wall of trees at the end of the field.

'Mind the branches.' V eases her way through an opening and I follow. I grasp slimy bark and move mossy boughs out of my path with cold damp hands. We thrash through leaves and step out from the thicket. In front of us is another field of trenches with mounds piled high like huge molehills. I blunder after V across this field and stop for breath. I'm tired from trying not to slide in sludge. Ahead is a hill, dotted with sheep and behind it a carpet of burnt orange trees. A distant church spire pokes through.

'Quickly!' shouts V when she sees I've stopped. She's looking up at the cloud moving across the sky. Again, I trip along after her. Reaching the edge of the field she disappears between the trees. I follow and find a clearing and a rubble path. Wild grass and thistle escape through cracks. A corrugated iron cabin stands in front of me, the door open. V sticks her head out. Strands of honey-coloured hair cling to her face and her cheeks are flushed.

'Quickly!' she repeats. I run in as the downpour begins and V slams the door behind us.

I catch my breath and look around uneasily. The cabin is dusty and smells of sawdust. In the far corner is a small window, specked with rain. The walls are smeared with dirt and footprints blotch the floor. A strip light and some plug sockets dangle loosely by their wires. I wonder where Dad's gone and how long I'll have to stay here.

'Are you cold?' V asks. I nod. 'No electricity. If health and safety came here they'd shut us down. But you can take one of those blankets.' Spades, hoes and muddy leather boots clutter the doorway.

The grimy blankets are heaped next to them. In the corner stand a table and some metal chairs. V unstacks the chairs and pushes one toward me. It scrapes against the stained floor, and a hollow echo fills the cabin. 'Sit down,' she says. I sink into the chair and try to wriggle my numb toes. I can feel insects crawling over me. They leave invisible trails across my skin. V sees me wincing. A vertical crease gathers between her eyebrows.

'Do you want to give me your coat?' she asks. She removes hers, and hangs it on one of four coat hooks, next to a noticeboard. My fingers fidget with my zip. 'Is it caught? I'll do it.' She helps me out of my coat and hangs it up. The gleaming macs drip down the wall creating a pool on the floor. She sits down next to me.

'Your mother should have given you gloves. No wonder you're cold. Do this.' She cups her hands and breathes into them. I copy, covering my nose and mouth with my fingers and watch her, wide-eyed. V has gleaming hair, pale skin and deep blue eyes. I've never seen a girl as pretty as her. I think she's perfect. I bet she had lots of friends at school when she was my age. It's not until much later that I notice her small flaws – bitten nails and traces of eczema around her hairline. I want to be her. I suppose she must be quite young, twenty maybe, although all adults seem old to me. She catches me gaping at her and laughs. I see her pondering this strange, quiet girl who looks and behaves younger than a twelve year old. I'm used to grown-ups looking at me like this.

'Not very talkative, are you?' I can't think how to reply so we sit in silence. I'm not sure if this annoys her. Outside, the wind howls and the shutter clatters against the side of the cabin. The handle on the door creaks and a man steps in. He pulls the door hard shut behind him. I stare at his stubbly face and deep-set eyes. 'Who's this?' he asks V, turning his back and shrugging off his coat. He runs his fingers through his drenched hair. There's a pencil tucked behind his ear.

'Stephen's daughter.'
'What's she doing here?'
'Mother's ill.'

Is Mum ill? This is the first I've heard of it. I look at V but she has her head down in a folder that she's removed from a rucksack. The man sniffs and removes the pencil from behind his ear. He scratches his head with it. Then he picks up a blanket and goes over to the rear of the cabin. Rolling back his muddied sleeves, he holds it up. I watch as he tries to fasten it over the gap between the glazed window and its metal frame. His outstretched arms are matted with hair.

'It won't stay,' says V. 'I've tried.' After a few attempts he throws it down and pulls up a chair next to her.

'This is going to take all day if the weather carries on. Whole site's waterlogged.'

'It'll let up soon.'

'So where's Stephen?'

'Gone to see the contractors.'

'Leaving his daughter? She looks half frozen. What's your name?' he asks me.

'Perdie,' I reply.

'Are you going to help us, Perdie?'

I nod. He smiles and reaches over, smoothing the back of my head with his palm.

'Your dad should've brought you along when we're excavating. She's going to have to watch us cleaning the trenches all day,' he says to V. V stands up and goes to the window. She leans her cheek against it and squints into the light.

'By the time we've written up, the rain should clear. There's blue sky over there.' She sits down again. Taking out some more folders, she passes one to the man.

I sit quietly listening to their pencils etching the paper. A comfortable silence settles over them that I'm not part of. I'm not supposed to be here.

'I've looked at the geophysical maps and there's nothing here,' the man says after a while.

'You might be right but there's a dark patch.' V turns a page in the folder and points at something with her pencil. The man leans over to look. 'Stephen thinks it could be a feature and we haven't checked that area yet.'

'He's the boss so he's got to be right,' says the man.

'I think he probably is right, Connor.'

'You would.'

V looks up from her folder. 'What's that supposed to mean?'

'All right, V, keep your knickers on.' The man half laughs.

V puts down her pencil and folder, stands up and goes to the window. 'It's only drizzling. Let's get on with it.'

I follow them out across the field. Though the rain is lighter, my legs and feet are freezing. My hair hovers in front of my eyes and my hood blows over my face. I feel spots of rain on my cheeks. The man and V stop and look back for a moment. He goes on but she stands and waits for me. I try to speed up but the mud sucks at my boots and forces me almost to topple. So I carry on more slowly until, in time, I reach her.

'You okay?' she asks. I nod, shivering, and wipe my wet nose with the back of my hand. 'I can't think why your mother sent you out in this weather. Your clothes aren't even waterproof.' V rubs her hands up and down my arms. She gives me an unexpected bright smile. 'Look, don't worry. See up there? Won't be long before the sun's out. Maybe there'll even be a rainbow.' Despite feeling miserably cold, I bask in the glow of her warm smile. 'Come on.' She takes my hand. 'Connor will think we're slacking.'

V is right: before long, the wind and rain die down and the sun appears. V suggests that I take a walk to keep warm so I pick my way around the nettled boundary of the field and tread toadstools and colourful leaves into the ground. I look down at V and Connor stooped over the trenches. Right now I feel more comfortable around them than Mum and Dad and I'm certainly happier than being trapped in a classroom with those girls. V waves over to me and shouts something. I stumble toward her.

'D'you want to help?'

'Yes,' I reply.

'Right, what you need to do is this. Are you watching?' She hoes the surface of the trench with light, easy movements. 'You have to keep it smooth. You don't want it lumpy and you don't want the darker clay to get mixed up with the lighter clay underneath so you need to be careful. D'you think you can do that?'

'Yes.'

I take the hoe from her and wipe away blades of grass and insects that float on the surface of the trench. Before long, the small of my back and tops of my arms are sore. My lips feel dry and my throat itches. The joints of my thumb and index finger where I hold the hoe throb but I soldier on, keen to impress V. If I do well, maybe I won't have to go back to school and can come and help again on Monday.

'You've done a good job, thanks,' says Connor a while later. I feel pleased until he starts to redo the area I've worked on. I sit on the canvas that they've laid out and watch V. She stops for a moment and secures her hair loosely with a pen and pencil. Then she stoops to dig. I gaze at the golden strands that feather out at the back of her head, as they catch the sunlight. I tug at a clump of my own red wiry hair and start to chew on it.

'What are you looking for?' I find myself asking.

'Nothing. We're just cleaning the site. Then we'll take a photograph to prove there's nothing here.'

'No one's walked on this boulder clay before we did so we know nobody's left anything to find.' Connor swipes at a fly that hovers near his face.

'According to your father the land's been disturbed in the next field, though. We've got to dig a few more trenches and have a look.' V stops and rubs her forehead with the back of her wrist. 'That's if we ever get round to it.'

'Who disturbed it?' I ask.

'Saxons, Normans . . . who knows? Could be people much further back. A Bronze Age woman and child were uncovered three miles away.'

Connor rests his spade upright and leans on it.

'And the A5, what's known as Watling Street, runs through here. Romans would've buried their dead along it to stop their spirits from returning home. We might unearth some of them although it's unlikely in my opinion.'

'You dig up dead people?' V sees me looking at her differently. She glances at Connor and giggles.

'We've dug up human remains.' I can see that she's enjoying the expression on my face. 'So has your dad. Anyway, we won't find anything if we don't speed up.' She moves to the end of the trench and I watch her slim figure as she works, outlined against the dark green field and the white autumn sky. I look down at the caramel-coloured stream that trickles through the clay at my feet and I think of what might lie below. I feel a chill travel down my spine. There's something wickedly exciting about uncovering things that are supposed to remain buried. I watch the cloudy water as it ripples in the breeze and a shadow falls across it. Connor is standing over me.

'Are you hungry yet? I think we've just about finished here.'

I scramble to my feet.

'Lunch,' Connor shouts over to V.

'We should carry on whilst the light's good. Stephen's not going to be happy if he comes back and finds us sitting around,' she shouts back.

'Well, his daughter's hungry.' V puts down her spade and makes her way over to us.

'I'm going to build a fire near the cabin; it's freezing,' says Connor.

'It's too damp. It won't kindle and we can't stop long. We need to get back up here before the light fails.'

'Come on, V, she's catching her death.'

'Go on then. You go ahead and see if you can get it started.' Connor throws a rucksack over his shoulder and strides off. He carries some spades with his slack arm. It seems that for him the mud is no obstacle. V goes down the hill with me, letting me set the pace. By the time we reach the bottom, smoke is curling up through the trees and the air smells of burnt timber.

'Looks like he managed to get it started. Don't tell your dad, will you, Perdie?' I sit down on a blanket next to Connor and let the heat warm my face and body. V kneels by my side.

'Marmite or cheese and tomato?' She takes a plastic bag from her rucksack.

'I'd like a bit of steak to barbecue over this – lovely,' says Connor.

'Sorry if my sarnies aren't quite to your taste.' V laughs lightly. She unwraps a foiled package and passes me a Marmite sandwich. I bite into it, floury bread coating my lips and crumbling inside my mouth. 'You could always do your own next time.'

'I'm sure they're delicious, V. What would I do without you?' Connor grabs a sandwich from her and takes a large bite.

'You'd have to find yourself a girlfriend to look after you and stop relying on your friends.' V and Connor hold each other's gaze. I'm embarrassed. V begins to pour mugs of tea and gives one to me. I hold it to my mouth and bathe my hands and face in the warm steam. As I drink, I concentrate my attention on the fire so I don't have to look at V and Connor. For a while we sit in silence and, slowly, a surprising feeling of contentment creeps over me. I realise I'm actually enjoying myself here with V and Connor. Somehow life doesn't seem so complicated when I'm outdoors. There's no Mum and Dad arguing. There are no girls calling me 'skinny' or 'weirdo' or 'new girl'. I'm free. This is one of those unusual moments when I'm not looking forward or back for happiness. I am happy – right here, right now.

V sighs. 'We're going too slowly. Stephen wants this finished within the next couple of weeks and we've got two more fields to go.'

'Don't worry about it. We'll get it done. He should hire more people if he wants it done quicker.'

'Maybe he can't afford it.'

'Maybe he's a tight git.' V glares at Connor as he tucks a thin cigarette between his teeth and lights it. He tilts his chin and breathes out. I watch his breath rising in the air.

'The sun's going down. I said it would. There's less daylight here than anywhere I've been – even when I worked up in Northumberland on that Uni placement.'

Connor looks up at the gloomy sky and the mist coming in over the hills.

'Yes, it's strange – probably something to do with being in a valley or maybe that fog is the spirits of Roman soldiers buried by the road?' He grins at me.

'Stop talking bollocks, Connor,' says V.

'Why so cynical?' he smirks. 'People say they've seen things. Could be down to overwork and lack of sleep but I'm open-minded.'

'You've had too many spliffs.' She reaches around me and cuffs Connor's shoulder. Connor turns to me.

'You believe in ghosts, don't you, Perdie?'

I stare at the fire. I imagine the people who have been here before me sitting with us now. Through the flickering flames, I see the Roman soldiers that Connor talks of. They're dressed in cloaks and roasting joints of meat. I hear spitting fat as they turn skewers and talk and laugh. Next to them I see the Bronze Age woman and her baby. The one that Connor said lies buried just over the hill. She looks at me with serious brown eyes and looks down at the child bundled in her arms. Her legs are curled up beneath her. She's only wearing a light brown shift and she's trying to keep warm. In this moment, these people feel closer and more real than anyone else and I like this hidden world that V and Connor are uncovering. I want to believe the people who have gone before me are still here.

'Yes, I do,' I answer gravely.

'Two out of three, V. You're outnumbered. Dozens of Romans probably died on battlefields near here. Their angry spirits could be trying to come back,' Connor says, ruffling my hair.

'All right, Connor, give me some of that.' V reaches across and takes the small cigarette from Connor's lips. She purses it between her own. Then she takes it out of her mouth, pressing it between her thumb and finger, and blows a jet of smoke into the air. I listen to the splutter of the fire as I furl locks of my hair around my finger and watch my imaginary Romans eat, behind the flames. The hills above us are now a blanket of dark trees. A low wind moans through their boughs. They hiss as if they are whispering to each other. I can see the field beyond the clearing. Earth is piled high all around, like burial mounds. I shiver. It's as though I've been standing alone in an unlit room and now the light has come on; I'm sharing my world with people from other ages.

A distant gunshot makes me jump.

'You okay? Just some hunters making the most of the last light,' says Connor.

'Yes.' I blink and stir myself as if I've been sleeping.

'We should pack up,' V says. 'The rain's going to start up again soon.'

I walk with them to the cabin, scuffing my soles against the gravel. I'm thinking about what Connor's said. I turn to look over my shoulder and see a figure in the next field. The person leaps over the fence, bringing his legs together above it, before landing. As he draws nearer, I recognise the stride.

'Stephen's here.' V is looking over my head. 'Can you get out the torch from the bag in the corner, before it gets too dark, Perdie?' She and Connor push past me. I go inside and begin to rummage through V's rucksack. I feel a cold round glass surface in between handfuls of woollen jumper. After a moment I hear Dad's voice.

'Looks like you've had that fire going for sometime. What time did you stop?'

'Only about half an hour ago. The light had gone,' Connor answers.

'Have you had a chance to check out that stretch up there?'

'Not yet,' says V.

'There's something up there, I'll tell you that.'

'We'll make sure we get round to it as soon as possible,' Connor responds.

I come out of the cabin clutching the torch and see the three of them standing by the fire. Connor and Dad stand – legs apart, centring their weight, hands in pockets, surveying the field. They seem to mirror each other. V stands between them, looking up at Dad. She appears smaller. I approach them and stand next to V.

'Can I come back with you tomorrow?' I ask her.

Dad turns his focus on V and me.

'I'm not working tomorrow, Perdie. It's Saturday.'

'Can I come back Monday?'

'You have school,' says Dad.

'I've missed school today.' Dad's expression is grim and I tail off.

'You can help another time,' says V.

She and Connor dowse the fire, gather their bags and start to head off. I wait in the dim light for Dad to lock up. As they move further off, I see Connor put his arm around V and she shrugs him off. They're arguing. I can hear their voices but they're too distant for me to make out. After a moment I realise Dad is watching too.

'Those two don't work well together,' he mutters, as we set off in the other direction, towards the van.

Anna Whitwham

Anna Whitwham was born in London in 1981. She has a BA in English and Drama from Queen's University, Belfast, and the University of California, Los Angeles. 'Red Brick Estate' is an excerpt from *Break Time*, a novel told through interlinking stories.

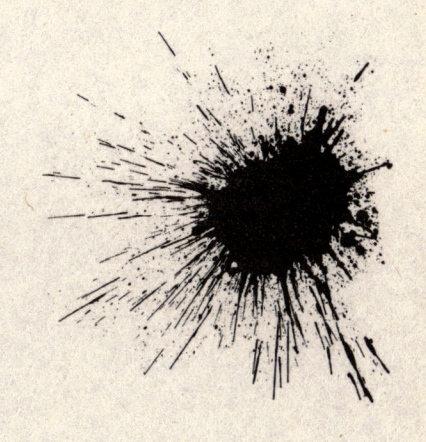

Red Brick Estate

The posh lady's cat sat on a wall. It blinked at Emily with moon-eyes, as Emily followed Julian. His stride was a lean, nervous gallop and she tottered behind him. She looked back to the cat, all plump and puffed fur as she stepped into the shadows of the red block of flats.

Julian pushed Emily hard against the wall of the lift. Her shoulder blades met as her back tensed up. They'd gone up three floors without saying a word, the silence only flickering as Emily unwrapped a packet of wine gums and popped an orange one into her mouth.

When he kissed her she hadn't finished swallowing it. She had to push it to the side of her gum quickly, before he used his tongue again.

He left a thick trail of wet mouth around hers. She swallowed the sweet. They took up silence again. Emily looked at the rippling metal floor of the lift and to the walls tagged with who had been there and when.

The lift was slow and tired. Emily wondered how many boys and girls it had carried. When they got to the sixth floor, Julian walked out taking her with him by her arm. They walked up iron stairs and halfway he stopped her, carefully put her bag down and kissed her again. She had to tiptoe, and was unsure of herself on the stair. He put a hand under her striped jumper and felt around. His hand was cold and unsure on her skin. Fingers and thumbs playing on her collar bone and rib cage. He moved down, around her bra, feeling the bow in the middle, the lace swirls on the cup, baggy because it held so little. Then he took his hand away. She gulped as he did and waited for the kiss to finish, too much saliva in her mouth. Her eyes opening every few seconds to see if his were closed.

He took her hand again and led her back down the stairs. Wordless they stood in the lift. Emily dabbed at her chin and upper lip with the back of her hand, trying to get rid of the spit, trying to do it so Julian wouldn't see. When they were at the bottom, Julian bent down and kissed her again, then jogged out into the open. Out of the Red Brick Estate.

Emily looked across the daylight and licked her lips, tasting him again. Lori was waiting for her outside the tube station. Where she'd said she'd be. She was sitting, beating her trainers on the wall.

She looked into Emily's face.

'Your lips are bright red, man.'

Emily took out her own packet of cigarettes, speaking with it held between her teeth as she looked for matches.

'He took me to the sixth floor.'

Lori gave her a lighter. 'I've only been first and second. Or in the archway.'

There was a pang in Emily's chest. Of hope that he might think her better, and of worry that he might think her worse than the others.

'You think he's ashamed?'

Lori folded her arms.

'I don't know what he thinks, do I?'

She walked, shaking her head at Emily being silly. Her shoulders twitching in the cold. She patted Emily on the arm with her right hand.

'I don't think anything.'

When they walked into school, Emily looked for Julian. He was by the lockers with Carl. She waited for him to smile first. He turned, a slight, quiet nod for her, separate from the streams of noise zigzagging around them. Emily played with the hoop in her left ear and smiled back. Then she and Lori popped into the toilets for a quick cigarette before registration.

Emily walked in and the mask of smoke already set by other girls made her wish she'd waited for her cigarette. Three of them from the year above lined the tiled wall. A fourth straddled the sanitary disposal bin. They stared hard at Emily; even through the stormy smoke they held their gaze. A fifth came out of a cubicle, pulling up the zipper on her too tight jeans. She pulled with the long hard false nail on the second finger of her right hand. Painted on the nail was a palm tree, the leaves studded with gold beads. She stared too, her blunt purple pencil scraped over her real lip line.

They all lit their cigarettes and Emily tried not to look their way, which was hard, because Lori had put her back to all of them. So Emily had to try and look at nobody in the scary quiet. Emily flicked ash into the sink and ran the tap to put it out. She looked into Lori's face, willing her to do the same. But Lori took another casual drag, leaning back on the sink, and Emily held the cigarette under water until it broke off, her head down.

Tamara had two waxy black ringlets on each side of her ponytail. She took her packet from the top of the hand dryer and held it between the tips of her fingers. She was silent as she walked up to Emily, her market gold bangles fading orange on her meaty wrists.

Her face had pulled itself into a look of pain. She had gold contacts in her eyes that burned underneath her Egyptian eyebrows. Her pupils slicing up Emily with each nasty careful blink. All inside the smoke of her eyeliner. She licked her plump, perfect lips and did a kind of smile.

'You just fucked Julian in the flats.'

Emily's face began to burn. Her chest was hot and itched under her jumper.

'No, I didn't.'

Tamara turned to the mirror and smoothed down the baby curls on her forehead stuck down with sweat and gel. She had time. She stepped closer to Emily, and pointed the palm tree finger at the glassy air next to Emily's head. Conducting her accusation. She slowed her voice down, but moved her lips hard and slow.

'You just fucked Julian in the flats.'

'No. No, I didn't fuck anyone.'

Emily's face ached with red. She itched in the smoke and the fear. She didn't know how to protest. Tamara walked slowly back to the wall. She turned to the girl on the sanitary bin.

'Girl's lying, you know. Hangs around with that slag and tries to lie. She's got dick written all over her face.'

Anna Whitwham

She turned back to Emily, her big hip stretching her spray-on jeans. The palm trees and gold rings of her right hand rapping on her thigh. She stared Emily out, and kept staring until Emily tearfully backed out of the toilets. Lori followed, blowing out her last bit of smoke from her mouth and her nose.

Emily ran all the way through the school and out of the gates. She ran all the way into the park, sat on a bench, her face in her hands. Lori put her left arm around Emily's shoulders and even though Lori was thin and smelled of damp, Emily fell into her, gripping her little waist with both of her arms. She cried. And Lori kept her left arm around her, sort of pulling away.

Lori left to go to the shop and get more cigarettes, leaving Emily alone. Emily stayed bent on the arm of the bench. She was frightened. She kept scrunching her eyes together to stop the crying. She worried about missing registration.

Lori came back ripping off the silver from a packet of Lamberts and held out a bottle of Coke for Emily.

'Drink it, fizz will stop you crying.'

Emily did as she was told. But after her first sip, she kept spitting on the ground as if she was going to be sick.

'What you expect?'

Lori sucked her cigarette and dried herself out a little more.

'You think people don't watch who's walking into the flats?'

Emily tried to breathe slower. She didn't like this hard lesson Lori was trying to teach her.

'People know what Red Brick's for. People see who goes in.'

Emily tried to find her voice again. It squeaked out, from the sobs.

'I don't know what I thought. This is not fair.'

Lori snorted. Her arms were bumpy in the cold, her light brown hairs raised. She still hadn't got a winter jacket because she was hoping for one of Emily's.

Emily whispered.

'But I'm not like you.'

Lori heard.

'Sorry?'

Emily didn't care. She raised her voice.

'I'm not like you. You heard them. They called you a slag. They think I'm like you.'

Lori sat very quietly, her lips blue. She sat huddled and smoking with her legs crossed, but her right patent heel was tapping quickly on the ground.

Because she said nothing, Emily carried on.

'I'm not one of them. I'm not one of you, I'm clean.'

Lori turned around, her face screwed up and grey. She spat in Emily's face. Spit swung on her lower lip and it stayed there as she finished her cigarette.

'Now you're fucking not.'

Emily dragged her shoulder bag after her as she walked out and slammed the gate. When she was out of the park, she turned back to Lori in tears. Lori was still cross-legged and smoking.

'Lori,' she yelled, 'I fucking well hate you.'

Lori stuck her middle finger high into the air and didn't even look her way. Then Lori turned slowly, and grinned. She stuck her middle finger even higher into the air.

'Not as much as I hate you.'

Julian found out. He took Tamara to the front gates. He had her by the wrist, pushing and pulling her as she struggled. In front of people too. Emily watched from a window in an art room, at the top of school. Tamara limped away wounded, not looking at anyone. The inside of her fat thighs rubbing at her jeans. She flicked away tears on her cheeks with her nails, stopping eyeliner smudging with the pad of her thumb.

Emily sneaked to the sixth form to use their toilets. Just until Tamara forgot. Leggy girls lined up against the tiled walls with shaggy nourished hair and cheekbones. They stared at Emily, charity shop beads around their swan necks and heavy hardback books in their bags. Their oversized velvet jackets were pinned down with vintage brooches and badges. They took out tobacco pouches filled with rolling paper, lipstick and loose change. Their beautiful gaze crawled over Emily as she walked out, drying her hands with the rough, pink paper.

Lori sulked for an afternoon. And the morning of the next day. Emily made peace in Tuesday afternoon's registration. She smiled over at Lori with slight shame and went over. Lori pretended like Emily wasn't there at first, marking up the form room desk with a leaking pen.

'You know I didn't mean it, right?'

'Yeah.'

The ink was all over Lori's middle finger.

'I'm sorry.'

'It's cool.'

Lori never apologised for spitting in Emily's face, but she gave her a cigarette and held Emily's arm all the way to the playground. She borrowed Emily's black wool coat for the winter, and never gave it back.

Emily kissed Julian in the flats for two weeks. Still they journeyed wordlessly. On each visit, Emily spat out her fruit gum before they got to the sixth floor. She wanted to make sure she tasted sweet and not of tobacco. A collection of orange and yellow balls started to build up in the corner of the lift.

One day, after school, they walked across the bridge to his Nan's flat. A plastic plant with chewed up tinsel wrapped round the stems and leaves stood next to the front door. Underneath the pot was one key. Julian held her hand as he let them in, and she tripped over the mat. His Nan was sleeping in front of the murmuring television when they got there, next to the fake fireplace. A row of peach-faced tree fairies lined the shelf above, next to glittering Christmas cards. The smell of baked ginger was still warm and spicy in the flat.

Julian lay Emily down on the mat in the bathroom and ran both the taps in the sink. He stroked her hair too quickly, pushing her fringe away from her eyes.

'If she wakes, I can say I was having a shower after football.'

Emily nodded and looked behind her at the woven basket next to the toilet filled with fat white toilet rolls.

Red Brick Estate

He made space by moving the washing rack and the drying blouse and skirt into the bath tub. He tried to kiss her as her jeans came off, slipping his tongue over her neck.

He was so black against the white bathroom. Against her. Her skin looked wormish now. She had a small bruise on her kneecap that she hadn't noticed before. It was tender and blue, and it glowed on the bone. The bare ceiling light fell on them. Her eyes stared at it too long and she blinked back the fizzing beads from the back of her eyes. She breathed in and felt them on the back of her throat and a dry, sharp push made her shut both eyes even tighter. The pain splintered to the edges of her back and belly and she let out one small whisper of noise.

Julian zipped himself up and went out to pour Emily a glass of orange squash, letting her get dressed. She pulled her knickers up quickly and pressed a hand to herself. She could feel a pulse. She was desperate for a wee. When she wiped, there was blood and she scrunched up a ball of tissue and stuffed it inside her knickers. She had pulled on her jeans by the time he came back. He was scratching his damp stomach and holding a glass out. She sat on the edge of the bath, sipping her squash as he ran his fingers through her long ponytail. Like their journeys through the Red Brick Estate, they said nothing.

There was a gold clock. Its metal sunbeams stretching on the green walls, with the minute hand stuck, ticking at three again and again. They left without his Nan waking, her lips loose and her chin wrinkled and wobbling as she slept. He had taken a slice of ginger bread for Emily and she wrapped it in the thick white toilet roll and put it in her pocket. He put the key back under the pot.

They stepped out into the late afternoon. Emily looked up and down at all the lace curtains drawn in all the windows. A man let his dog off the lead below and it ran to a girl in a puffy coat. He roared, telling the dog to come back. The girl squealed and ran to her bored-looking mum, who pushed another child on the swings with one arm. Julian tried to hold her hand as they walked, but Emily put them in her pockets and felt the ginger bread sitting there. When they got to the bottom she told him she could find her way back to the bridge fine.

She walked over the river and felt cold. The evening was coming in a dark plain grey. She stopped and looked at the sickly water and scum on the river's brown banks. She stood twisting the ring on her thumb, getting colder.

Emily showed her pass to the driver, but didn't make eye contact. She sat on the bus home with a headache, trying to doze with her cheek to the greasy window, but the bus rumbled loudly and the pain down there groaned and made her want to go to the toilet again. There was a young woman sitting opposite. Emily took out her ponytail and shook her hair out; it was too tight on her scalp. They got stuck in a traffic jam and the woman looked up, raised her eyebrows and shook her head. Emily smiled back, but she felt tears behind her eyes where those beads of light had been. She wanted to hold the woman's hand to steady herself. She wanted to tell this woman that she had just done it. But the woman looked like she'd had a tiring day herself.

They had chicken for dinner. Emily chopped her meat slowly, staring hard at her plate, Julian's sweat dry on her body. She pushed her legs tightly together, squeezing her thighs shut. Her mum said she looked pale, ran her a bath and gave her a plate of chopped apple.

As the bath ran, Emily phoned Lori. She told of her afternoon in patches, skipping over some stuff for now, embarrassed by her blood and pain. Lori asked if it felt good and Emily said it felt weird. Then Lori asked if she had bled and Emily had half a slice of apple in her mouth that she had to finish. Lori waited in the silence until Emily swallowed and said to Lori that she had, but only a little. She was scared that Lori knew too much now. That she'd have to be extra nice to her tomorrow.

Emily crossed her legs over another dull twinge and her foot caught the handle of the cup. Emily watched it fall and roll onto the Turkish rug, the tea seeping into the red carpet underneath.

She made Lori swear, with hand on her heart, not to say a word to anyone about anything.

'Please, Lori.'

Emily waited in Lori's silence and heard her breathing out smoke. When the smoke was all gone, Lori laughed and said of course she'd keep it a secret. She swore on her life and the lives of everyone she knew.

Polly Atkin

Polly Atkin was born in Nottingham but moved to London to study English at Queen Mary College. After graduating in 2002 she stayed in London, and now earns her living writing, teaching and performing.

Bone Song

Though it was   a pub in Deptford
and no blood-washed   hall of heroes
built from battle   spoil of monsters
strung like skin   from rib-cage arches
held up high   by thigh-bone pillars,
when the harpist   sang her songs
it seemed her harp   was made of bones
and strung with sinew   heart strings   gut
so when each chiming   chord was plucked
the harp bones hummed   a deathly drone.
I felt its voices   own my own
as though it sang   my own bone song.
My heart-valves hammered   thorax rang.
The harpist stood   the harp was wood.
I'm still singing   bones and blood.

Polly Atkin

Room

I dream of the room we will wake in, one day,
after we've painted it into a forest

long lean limbs of silver birches
growing to greenwood over our heads

and the risen sun, warm as a finger-tip, touching
its eyelash-fine wings on our opening faces

brushing our eyes into pools, catching light,
and stippling the ceiling with sky-looking flickers;

paths to the blue air beyond the high leaves,
and all around, drawing us out from the walls

the spaces
between the trees.

Stockholm Syndrome

I hated the school, its meanness, its stench
of disinfectant, dogs and last week's dinner,
how the looming old house vibrated on brown
and squeaked like polished lino,

the way the boys would shove you around
in the playground, the way you were always to blame
no matter who bashed into who, who spoke
out of turn, who threw the potatoes.

And yet I would find myself, after I left,
climbing a tree to post notes through the air-vent
in the library wall that sided our garden,
or stood on a bank peering over the fence

where the plum trees hid me from the eyes of the house
on my side, from the crouching classrooms on theirs,
where the leaves underfoot were as deep as autumn
and the scrawny fox made his den.

Polly Atkin

Mr Magpie

I met a magpie.
>   The magpie told me
'don't expect him to be there, young lady'
and flew off into the yellow trees
leaving no doubt.
>   It made it easy
to be there not waiting for him to see me
knowing I can't keep on watching for him
every time
>   when just that night
I'd dreamt he'd gone, while I transformed
bone after bone into tumbling stones
and fell
>   carried on falling till dawn,
when the greying light at last revealed him
there, where he had always been,
beside me.
>   But this was still a dream;
roads queued up to be driven before waking,
twisted and pinched into infinite circuits
we had to travel
>   unable to exit,
fighting about problems that never existed,
until the shock of an actual morning
alone.
>   So later walking home
when Mr Magpie landed before me
ominous, beady-eyed, cawing his warning,
I laughed
>   and carried on.

My Scotland

You must be my Scotland, only you do to me
what a first sight of Scotland does to me –
something unique in the beat of my heart,
no picture-postcard wild heathered hills scarred
WELCOME TO   VISIT   COME BACK SOON
but the thing it does, that thing you do

to know I am travelling, will be arriving
into a place that is also inside me –
from the bridge-spanned grey of the tarnished Tay
via East Neuk of Fife, firths of Forth and Moray
Ecclefechan Kircaldy Eastriggs and Scone
do to me things like that thing that you do

bitter but soft as a Solway morning
subtle but rich as a Galloway gloaming
Loch Morar deep and Ben Nevis high
wide as a world-wide Mid-Lothian sky
something both wonderfully extra and ordinary –
you do it, and do it to all of me.

Polly Atkin

The Cemetery on Wilford Hill

It is long long ago that white cold morning
I crawled to the foot of the bed, to the window
and saw it, right at the edge of the garden,
caught it out, almost half-way to the house –
shrapnel of gravestones, black in the snow
like scree on the hillside, row after row
and the hill itself, looming, terribly close.
Did it think I wouldn't take notice? know?
Not stir to the grate of stone on stone
as I slept, the crunch and grind of bones
as the dead picked up their legs and crept
inch by inch to where we lay
like death, but not – not ready yet –
nor feel the dragging wake of earth
as the ship, the hill was, broke its berth
and tried to break us like a wave
beneath it. This was long ago.
It changed tack when I told it to,
and never trespassed on our sleep
again, but there are times I've sensed
movement back behind the trees,
those summer evenings, thick with heat,
forgetful with it. Still, I know
that slither of grave-grey stone; the hill
blank and bitter with snow.

Unfurled

The sculptress runs her careful touch
over the swelling-smooth belly, feels
movement, shifting, under the membrane,
catches the tremulous pulse in her palm,
knows it is ready. Still, the cold stone
fights against giving its child to the light;
to let the air finger its delicate features,
to offer its terrible newness to death,
so the unborn creeps backwards, buries its face.
The sculptress turns surgeon, opens the skin,
beckons the bird, flapping soul, to the surface,
cradles its twisting form in her hands,
holds it tight, chisels away at the surplus,
cutting an exit, a clear open path
for an opening eye, a nose, a mouth,
a half-born angel, young as the world,
emerging from stone; shown, not made –
its flowing hair, its one arm raised,
its one freed wing, unfurled.

Polly Atkin

Xmas Fog

The fog dropped by on christmas eve
licking the tops of the houses to nothing,

wrapping its fat lips round the black trees
and sucking them down to spindles, pricking

star-like holes in the cushion of its tongue
so that night, like saliva, dripped down from above,

syrupy thick with the madness of sugar
sticking us all, like old sweets, together.

Apparition no. 3

It leaps at me out of the dark of the landing
a jack-in-the-box, sinister visitor. I jump back
almost missing a step, half fall. Is it

dear god it's the baby!
out of its cot, climbing onto the table
about to tumble over the banister, about to

No, it's just a balloon;
a purple balloon on a white plastic stick
planted askew in an old brass vase,

a peculiar fruit, a great big berry
swollen with juice, on a single stem.
I catch myself, ease on up to bed,

double-check the baby
gate behind me; squeeze the shadow
scene from my eyes.

Polly Atkin

Tree Dreams

If I hold my twig-brittle finger bones tight
in a fist, my knuckle bones rise up white;
stub-buds of new limbs, pressing my skin.

They hover close, under the surface, wait
for a signal, trigger. They itch for the light
and to move in it, grow to it, drink it all in.

They are greedy. I glimpse their dreams some nights,
dreams of branches, galaxies wide,
of fruit like planets, seeds like suns.

I frisk myself for gnarls and twists,
read each bone-knot as a sign, it's time
to change, the spring has come;

they shoot from me like splinters, scythes,
leave me skin-split like a pip and rise rise rise

Cleo Bartholomew

Cleo Bartholomew currently works with people with learning disabilities as a gardener in West Norwood. These poems are taken from her sequence *The Fisherman's Wife*.

After Work

October 16th, 1965, Porthgain, Wales

       Leaning into late afternoon talk
a laze – flicking paint – blue and white daggers – off
the shop windowsill with their thumb nails
                              the three of them,
still wearing wet boots, just paid, swap words, backchat.
Smiles glint in the sun like a collection of chipped marbles,
the battle scars of worn jokes, brought out, catch light:
                              glass balls clink,
colliding, sent rolling into each other, knocking scatterings,
cannon shinings of solid bubbles in all directions, the go of talk
moving on, from a fight in the market to the boats left behind
    them.
                              Their backs slant
into the porch like shadows. Tea – passed round tails out
tousled steam sun-sets, they mouth silk-wafts of smoke
expanding clouds, blond and blue cocoons, rise up.
                        He sips slowly
hands warming, closed on the cup. Loafing, already in his mind
thoughts of leaving, the moment floating and full, runs away
    from him
travels out and comes again, like a plastic bag tumbles in the
    tide.

Cleo Bartholomew

Supper

October 16th, 1965

>   Her back to him.
> He shuts the door, she starts again, the table spreads
> with green petals, curled, like unpeeled thumbprints
>   dropping   one by one   from her hands
>   from each sprout.
> The underleaves emerge, closed up tightly as a baby's fist.
>   (The pair of them are alone in the house.)
>   There will be too much food for two, again.

At the Dance

July 3rd, 1958, the church hall

Her slow walk was fluid unfurling as a story beginning
    across the hall – each step towards him
    like a palm smoothing velvet against the pile
    brushing a low roar of colour   static
as the crackle of gramophone music   humming thick
as date syrup on your finger tips
or a lover's spittle

    her slow walk
        so fluid   unfurling
            like his story
                beginning

Cleo Bartholomew

Walking Up the River

July 4th, 1958

Nets held in one hand

            his toes
                      splayed
sink
    through mud almost too soft with silt
to dare to wade   at the bottom
insect bites of broken mosaic   shell pieces prick
gravel-like   and sticking
nestle in the crease of the soles of his feet

heading towards the fork   bare-legged   with trousers rolled
stork-walking he delicately   picks
a path   away from the bank
        tied round the back of his neck   boot laces dangle
          a white ribbon flickers on his nape in the sunburn
        his head
              bowed
                    the thought

                                    he might see her again

The Missing Place at the Table

October 16th, 1965

While her back is turned the child draws a house
with lollipop flowers and scalloping clouds

a red chimney puffs small billows of blue smoke
spiralling slowly out, across the sky.

When she faces the window she can see the child
behind her, hair flat, ironed to a dark shine

and parted into two neat curtains tied back
over her brow. The small face bent over the picture

fades then changes; someone sighs, but the woman
doesn't hear; the sprouts boil over, the child

doesn't hear. Through the window, the day
red, a sucked peach stone, a swollen eye

too dry to cry or close turns, restlessly
rolling a rim of eye bright over the hills

until night like a gentle thumb presses it shut.
He waits. The food is done and again she brings

her hunger to the table to share and swallow:
Love says, you must sit down and taste my meat.
One after the other they add salt, and eat.

Cleo Bartholomew

A Second Meeting

July 10th, 1958

He jumps the field gate,
flipping like a duck
dives down, head first
feet swinging tail-up.

The banged lock rings out,
shaken steel cold bars
clang in his gripped hands,
metal sings in his arms.

Over-turned nettles,
green tall tower blocks
shake white flower lights
up, above the crop

into the blue sky,
wind-river passing by
him hung, swaying-still,
a black flame quivering

in the sun, bright behind
morning high. Vaulting up
he lands by the roadside,
thudding down, ground-struck

jarred by the cracked mud
heat baked, summer hard:
the yellow sea of hills
swells, and slowly calms.

Field-dazed by the corn,
he turns, and looking round
sees her across the road
standing, rippling in a haze:

the air is dense with simmering,
a murk of under-tree dark,
breathing in too much
his nostrils dry with dust,

his mouth works, swallows
to make more water,
drinking up, tiny ducts
click a frog song of saliva.

The road is a rind
of grey moon peeling,
bald and uneven
in front of his feet;

leaf shadows mingle
like lily pads lapping;
the soles of his town shoes
clap stiffly on the surface

too loud on the tarmac
in the quiet between them.
He walks on islands
that move, floating under him

across to the other side;
flattened green blades
splay out grass star rays
on the foot-worn tussocks

around the bus stop.
He stands two steps away,
behind her facing up the road
to where the bus first shows:

the two of them wait.
She puts a hand
in her coat pocket
and searches the lining.

A finding. She draws out
something and holds it
up, low, in front of herself
and out of his sight.

He moves his head
and looks over her shoulder
the silver magpie flash
of an opening mirror –

in the flipped-up lid
of her eye shadow compact,
one tiger-striped iris
black centred, looks back.

Digging

March 3rd, 1966

She stamps down on her spade
a clod fall of wet mud
from her boot on the ground
smacks in the after rain,
clumps drop back again.

The tail of her headscarf
flaps in the wind, a bird
has flown down and folded
grey long feathered wings
together under her chin.

Another tug pulls her sight
into flight from the hill,
hooks close on her clavicles,
high in the wide spring
bird dot and woman ride out

shrunk to a black skirt
swinging, below moving wings
a silhouette butterfly
winking further away
getting smaller, and smaller

a keyhole in the sky.
She passes over meadows,
on the hillside far below
an insect twitches, then stamps
on the soil like a drinking ant,

Cleo Bartholomew

moving away from the house
rows of turned over heapings
push up like mattress springs
following the little figure
digging in the garden.

The surrounding fields twirl round,
rutted brown and fodder green
turn a shawl swirl of patches
held together by hedgerows,
then the wind changes, out to sea.

Janet Irving

Janet Irving was born in Johannesburg, and studied English and Environmental Science at the University of Cape Town. She tutored English at the University while conducting research on Flannery O'Connor for a Master's degree. A scholarship for a postgraduate publishing course at Oxford Brookes University brought her to the UK. She currently lives near Oxford and works in academic publishing.

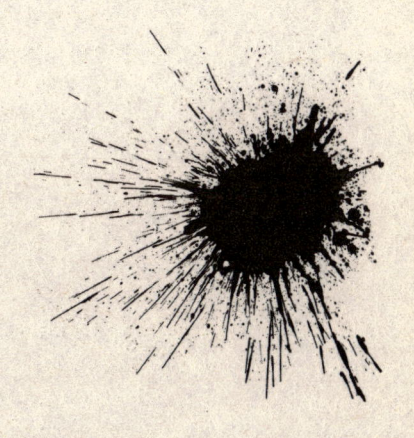

Purple Birds

The purple birds, crested, paired, turn out to be violet turacos.
Not residents, nor seasonal visitors, the expert said. Blown
off course. Slipped out from behind bars. Or simply lured
by the bright pickings of this urban forest. Johannesburg,
a swell of trees on jutting ribs, mainlined to distant waterfalls.
Once this upland flowed with grasses from baked rock-rims,
dusting the air with seed.

                                          The pair float on a telephone wire
against a strong bare sky. Lifted into column space, page nine;
our garden, my father, acknowledged. Guests from up north,
from Africa's belly; blood-tied to louries of Botswana's thigh,
Knysna's foot. Here, assuming a vantage point. Testing
the thin thirsty air, taking the high ground. *Makwerekwere*.
See, they no longer seek out shadowy canopies. Only their calls
are deep with the leaf litter of origin. They're out in the open,
showing off their shades.

Lourie – the South African term for a turaco.
Makwerekwere – a pejorative term in South Africa for immigrants, in particular those from other parts of Africa.

Janet Irving

Hibiscus

The hat bought in haste shorted the live-wire strands.
A pull-on with flaxen plaits, which, I was told,
turns me Scandinavian.

But in that charged Edinburgh afternoon, as the year
cartwheeled towards a big-screen finish, I saw myself
many latitudes south:

nattily plaited, freckled. A few loose filaments, blonde,
fine with salt, gesturing. I'd weave together
the crimson flowers

for the Christmas table; they'd find their way into our hair,
flushing our faces before they fluted –
a fold of night wings

taking in the colour. In runaway mornings,
they were kites catching in the height, the bite, of leaves,
in the serrated green

of summer. I'd stretch for the red – draw myself to a centre.
Find new-year intensity – oxygen –
unscented.

Angolan Sable

Hippotragus niger variani

'TECHNOLOGY ENABLES DISCOVERY – LEGENDARY ANTELOPE
NOT EXTINCT'

        You bend an infrared ray
break
     an imperceptible line
                a vein.
                   Meet
                      the edge.
             One shot
and you're fixed
         spread in pixels.

             One sample
and you're splintered
         sequenced.

Thirty years of elusion –
                of manoeuvring through
thickets, shadows
         blackened clearings
a thinning
        and sparking world
                  a bush-war.

Reappearance now:

Lifting your heads
         blood-dark

Janet Irving

                          marked
    sculpted
           to take the weight and height
of arching horns
                    scimitar lengths
    spiralling
        behind
                beyond
through the light
          the heat
like the wires
        shrill whistles
                    of waves
            carrying
unravelling
                  their own design.

Zomba

From the Malawi *sequence* (i)

I bite
into cassava –

flesh milks
through teeth,
dust-skin sticks:
a latching bat.

The vegetable seller
in purple, red,
jugs her hands,
offers more –

The president's face
leafed by stars
twitches
on her printed dress.

Sunk in shade
at Zomba's base
eight hard boots
of friends –

Whip-track
to the summit
before dark.

The day
on our back.

*

Janet Irving

I had steadied heels, packs
in Mt Mulanje's pre-dawn.

Pressed into light –
soft, then sharp.

Pushed on, against
the sky.

Bent
into the slope, the earth,
gathered the mesh:
obligatory skirt.

Blinked,
bit on straps,
as men jolted past:
the sweat
the shoulders
the hand-sawn planks.

Pulled on thoughts
all the way down.

Tested a line.

Tightened my grip
for the hours ahead:

the north-west road
the stop-starts
the sun-weighted bus.

The next leg.

*

I hold on
for the end
in the lurch of the day

hold on
for the top
in the high pitch of dusk

hold
to the skree

hold off
the tails

hold on
for the sign

the sight

a fire

a fire
with jaws
to hollow out
the night.

Janet Irving

Monkey Bay

From the Malawi *sequence* (ii)

We wake
to a shock
of white.

The spin
of a room.

No blue –
no tent
to touch.

Four beds,
light
off the glide,
slap of the wall.

Nets overhead
knotted
by other guests.

Torched struts,
spokes
of a fitful roof.

Hot tin,
our voices,
cracking.

We let you
sleep in –

a bed
for your birthday.

Your
long, lit back
finds the camber

inclines
to air –

reed to wind –

draws out
the stare.

Janet Irving

Thumbi Island

From the Malawi *sequence* (iii)

Oars
stretch the water
as we make
our way over.

The lake
is membranous –
a rippling
snail foot
lifting the nub of land.

Our boat shudders
over the threshold
of rock and branch –
we stretch, squint,
quiver
in the noonday green.

The fire-fish lunch
singes
our throats –

I back into the water
to take it in again
and speed becomes my air,
the far shallows
my light.

Limbs extend,
entice the sky
to the lightning below:

flints of tail, whipping tips,
the glassy flashes
of *mbuna* shoals.

For instants
their iridescent skins
paint my own, strike
the flaws. I'm caught
in the daub of a dance.

Janet Irving

Visitation

Heron Island, Great Barrier Reef

For the unborn

We're in the mouth of midsummer:
the squamous inside-cheek of noddy terns,
of fanning sky, pink and ridged,
dealing out the cries, the time,
the hungry air, the call of water,

the underwater whorls as corals whistle,
kiss the current, warm to quilling fins,
a silky wordless spell, the mesmery
of liquid light, turquoise breath,
the depth, the rise, the breaking

into a dousing heat, a late-day weight,
the giddy sway into forest hums and flashes,
a tipping of the hours, a glinting
leaf-laced ceiling gashing with the wind,
with dreams, a new sky bearing down,

day losing its edge, as dusk blows in
a thousand summer ghosts, the sea-struck
mutton birds, whose hollow songs
lift the bones of waves, of sleep,
cool the peaks, bring an old word close –

spookvoël – in softer moments, my sister's
name, a child called forth by late-night

whoos, and now a generation on, uncurled,
I reach through the charge, the chorus,
for you – my eye-ember, my shudder.

Spookvoël, 'ghost bird' – the common Afrikaans name for the secretive Grey-Headed Bush Shrike

Kate Miller

Kate Miller studied History of Art at Cambridge and Fine Art at Central St Martin's. In 2005 she won the Southwark Poet of the Year competition and the PFD student award. She lives in London and works as a gardener.

Colour Beginnings

Sketchbook CCLXXXIII: the Burning
of the Houses of Parliament

Up all night, until the wind changed,
with but four colours to hand.
At seven on the Strand smelled smoke, fancied
I heard Trojans in the firecarts' bells.

Filled my flask at the Adelphi steps
and hailed Old Booth. He rowed the tender
crabwise across the Lambeth mud,
secured it and scuttled off. Tide out,

mud and hawsers bronzed in the furnace light.
Before me blazed the last trump or sunset on the Nile,
those burning Houses a foreign fleet.
I've seen every yellow Earth can conjure,

yet I had only one, and though I've made it match
a sunrise, brimstone, saffron, sulphur,
even jaundice, I thought it insufficient here –
those palaces were cracked crucibles, leaking red gold.

Just as well I had the fierce vermilion
since Everyman above me on the bridge
was tanned a redskin, African, Indian,
joining the procession from our dominions.

From under stovepipe hats and shawls swelled
a great stare of faces, leonine, upturned red
earthenware, roaring, *There, Sirs, go your Reforms!*
White bonnets were like helmets, some bloodied.

Kate Miller

All this I got down, scribbled, sponged, stained.
Yet I wished there was a better black than lamp black
to serve for that charred mass, damned dark
the orange tongues had lapped, ash, soot, slag.

Up-lit throughout the night the sky demanded blue,
more blue, a pan of cobalt – fire-bright,
smutted, greasy. I smeared it with my thumbs
and Ma Booth's cloth – that wrapped a pie,

hid it in the bailer, till I'd need of it –
This morning, flood the sheets anew to find
cinders, blown downwind, left scorch marks
before the paint had time to dry.

Drawing in King's Wood

I tread a floor padded with leafmould
to soften flints, turned when the charcoal kiln was built.

I'm brandishing the fat black sticks
and lumps of chalk, damp in the hand.

Gloom spills from a dry apse behind the hall of yew
where sunlight seldom shuttles in a web.

I'll grind a hill of charcoal into pools of shadow.
My brown paper is from pulp: the forest's own

sweet chestnut: I've smoothed the sheet down flat
as matting, earth-coloured beneath the trees' green soffits,

when, swift as falling, a deer vaults
off the forest path, lights up the glade

with fur, legs, the flare of her white scut.
Marks patter on the roll of paper, laid

down like Raleigh's cape. She bounds
into buff bracken, leaving her page behind.

Kate Miller

Emergency Landing

Ground corals slip between my toes,
cowrie grains swim in my shoes.
Please God let me wake up safe today.
I want to know the colour of the sand –

sand I have to step back on to see
the turquoise sea, the palm trees standing
straight, not crashing sideways
as we hit the ground.

There is a moment in the circling plane
when we look down and find
the ocean playing with a rope
of emeralds around its throat.

My mother's green eyes fix on one,
enlarging, as on prey. It has a landing strip,
wet at each end with waves, men piling fish.

Faces tip towards us, in the air, singing
or calling on Allah? In an instant dusk
has come and closed the curtains
like a nurse, snapping shut
the lid of lilac sky.

We can't all hold Mummy's hand.
Behind her seat we clutch our bears,
heads pushed down for the plunge,
My sister cries, is sick, more tears,

a stink. We hit the runway
rearing up. Stop, oh stop!

At last when we uncurl,
the air is cool.

After the ocean's stare,
we cannot lift our eyes,
but let them hug the ground.
We steer shy of hands,

to help us off the beach,
white in the torchlight,
and we are put to bed,
only to dive again in sleep.

Kate Miller

Souvenir of the Walrus

Before helicopters with gimbal mounted cameras,
it was eyes that travelled, trained to focus in all lights
across the floes. There was one famous hunt,
recorded on this horn, presented to the elders
when the men came home.

Here are the hounds running after elk.
Arrows pierce the stag, see, the marks
stop short: he sinks into snow, entering the cloudy
white where earth meets heaven – same colour
as the walrus tusk.

Men and boys with backpacks run towards
a bush-tail dog pulling at the throat of upturned kill,
watched by a hawk, stiff, still on a post.
Two curved beavers skirt the camp
upwind, low and long,

hump-backed as the storehouse roof.
Women climb the frame to lash down skins,
stacking the fish and meat brought back by sled,
to be smoked or cured, while the salt lasts,
or packed hard down in ice.

Turn it over: here are boats – paddled, or hauled
to open water – single sculls and longboats
with up to seven crew, some heaped with cargo.
Flotillas of bigbeaked birds bob by, platoons
of cranes fall in behind.

This is the walrus, enormous, half-drawn because
half submerged. A hunter on all fours faces the bull,
like burly man and wife across a table,

lets fly the harpoon, kills, ropes the carcass to a sled.
Two men slide it miles overland,

the length and satisfaction of the journey home
spun out along this tusk, in homage. As we hand it on,
spirit-creature, hear our prayer, grant us good sea harvest,
fill our females and yours with young – hardy, sharp-sensed
and fat enough for life on ice.

Kate Miller

Curfew

My Lord will call a curfew in the streets to night.
Oh my waiting women in blue, sing me to sleep
with words for colours of your home country.

Give me words to catch a moonflower opening,
the pink pipful of a pomegranate beneath its hairy leaf,
snores of a dog replete on field rabbit, snick of a swallow

as it shears through silk water held in a cistern.
All day I waited by the river, where the bank curves,
in the slow mudspot where I watched egrets

as a child, before irrigation channels cut through
lines of poplars. There I had wild flowers to untangle
but I missed the chatter of the laundresses,

the glitter of our fountains. When at last my love came
it was dark. He took me to a hedge-hollow
full of spines. I heard water sighing from below that hedge.

Give me my shift and veil, and mark the rising star.
Tell me the colours of your brothers' eyes,
tell your tales of the mile-long camel trains.

Sing of wide-open country, rock and scree, of dune dwellers
and your forebears in the high mountains. Women in blue
around a well, give me your words for the coldest blue,

the wall paint of your cities, of bolts of cloth dyed
blue as the eyes of Northern women
that your fathers kissed, opened to the skies.

Gillian Petrie

Gillian Petrie, now in her seventies, read English at Oxford. For thirty years, she worked in the hospice movement: as head of Marie Curie's national home nursing service; as a founder-trustee of Nairobi Hospice, Kenya; and as founder-director of Polish Hospices Fund, which organised training for Polish doctors. Ten years ago, she started to write with Kick Start Poets of Salisbury. She has two sons, two daughters; is married to Professor Muir Hunter QC.

Baskets

Weave the green and sinuous withies
from the cloudy Langport levels,
fit to bear a plaited bloomer,
hollow head of yellow pumpkin,
candles shining through the smile,
celebrating Hallowe'en;

overlap the strands of raffia,
stripped from palm trees by the ocean:
flaunt voluptuous mango, pawpaw,
ugli fruit and pomegranate,
on the high road to Nyeri,
steeply falling to the Rift;

tautly weave the mournful sackcloth
cut from Ganges delta hemplands:
carriers for herbal potions,
cures for dhobi itch and palsy,
dumdum fever, sleeping sickness,
broken hearts and broken minds;

scythe the reeds that smell so sweetly
of the tilth on Salthouse marshes;
dredge the wetlands where the curlews,
needle leggéd, brake their landings,
skid on water, agitated
by the gun-fire closing in.

Gillian Petrie

Master Builder

I walk about the house: I leave
my imprint on the jamb of every door;
close the shutters perfectly designed
never to knock the slender glazing-bars.

Do you admire the great saloon
in Adam-green, the ceiling rose restored,
the felling of the sycamore
that undermined the footings?

I planted sweetly-smelling small-leaf lime.
You will know this tree: *Tilia cordata*:
Grinling Gibbons' leaves and flowers,
viols and curlicues, inspired you.

I have left untouched many things
you crafted in your plainer joinery:
the curving baluster, the children's slide,
the doors askew within their architraves.

The fanlight holds the flawed prismatic glass
you fitted when you built the house
two hundred years ago: you know
it throws a pattern on your marble floor
like fantail doves in flight.

When he arrives, the next custodian
of your house – guide his hands
as you have guided mine.

Demurrer

i.m. David Kelly

Shame walked with him between the hedgerows
up towards the cusp of Harrowdown,
treading bracken, early afternoon,
rain in the air.

He had not met such plunderers before –
they made him break his own belief,
snapped his spirit like a twig,
strung him up.

Nonetheless, it moves.
It's calm up here at Harrowdown.
In their house, below, she is asleep –
thank God she is asleep.

Here, Iraq,
your weapons of destruction:
pills, a kitchen knife –
no threat.

Gillian Petrie

Between the Walls

Between the eastern and the western walls,
a great parterre was laid, a geometric quilt
of scented roses, gold and pink:
Hebe's Lip, *Celestial*, *Peace*.

Limbs draped over the apple-tree,
I look with yearning over the wall
at the asylum, monumental, yellow brick,
flowerless place, where patients stoop
and shuffle; others of their kind,
ploughmen, joiners, weavers, flutes,
work the fields, fashion things
in wood and cloth, break the chalk
to make the graves.

I never spoke the language of the west,
learned from those on the eastern side
how to submit and how to grieve –
I watched them from my tree.
                                   Even now,
digging the tilth a span too deep,
I turn up flints beneath the soil,
arrowheads too sharp for my own good.

In the Scanner

I won't look up –
never by a flicker –

>go to your cathedral
>calm crusader,
>lie upon your table tomb –
>whippet at your feet –
>gaze upward –

the atmosphere
within the metal coffin
palls –

>steel yourself to soar –
>touch the vaulting –
>feel how tender
>years of rising candle-smoke
>have made it –
>listen –

I hear the growling
of the haruspex,
bourdon to the higher melody –

>the plainsong of the choir –
>from side to side
>treble voices answer one another –
>point and counterpoint –

he uses lodestone
to extort the secrets
of the skeleton –
locusts pattening
on the bones –

>beyond –
>out on the plain –
>alien hands have drawn

Gillian Petrie

                                        wonderful patterns in the
                                           body of the corn.

The seer
may find the gap
between the walnut
and the skull
where shameful fungi
lie –

a foreshadowing of death –

                                        at last
                                        the sweet intake of breath.

Dreaming of Light

>   for my daughter, Sarah, who is autistic

the house
is different from the other thing
called house

the bed
is soft   it has a mother-smell
I sleep

the light
is all around   sounding
like the light

that licks
the bluish water into white
sips

the waves
sighing between the toes
tastes

of salt
blowing across the face
and hair

sings
of sun and sea and sky
and air

the song
when I awake is gone
words are lost

Gillian Petrie

this light
does not taste like the colour
of that light

is not
a sighing or a singing
light

Grief in Wlodawa

Ravens agitate the poplar trees
lining the road across the Pomeranian plain,
the conquerors' corridor;

a river bank, a
grassy bridge, bisected by a single wire,
mark the border;

on the western side,
furrows turned by horse-drawn plough
rule the earth.

Beyond the wire,
mist obscures the empty marsh,
bird-less sky.

The light fades
in the hospice chapel
as the child dies.

Grandmothers –
she and I –
weep.

Gillian Petrie

Tomfoolery

Suspended like a lesser star, the brooch
glows sulkily against the dark material,
bulbous gemstones red as Mars,
green as Cassiopeia's chair;
satellite ear-rings sway in space;

wrapped in the cloying atmosphere
of *Chypre*, she spirals through the tango
to the beat of Vic Sylvester; after every ball,
the scabrous comets are entombed
in velveteen.
                A hundred years before,
Mr Pinchbeck brooded over alchemy:
sweltered in his smelting house;
poured the bright Promethean stream
into heated crucibles – blending baser ores
with nobler – skimmed and burnished
the amalgam, pimpled it with cabochons.

Now the dancer flaunts her signal-lights:
fingers rubellites when she is tired,
strokes the olivines when she is not.

Silver Mine

Think of that summer at day-break,
the run through the grass in the early sun
to our secret lake in the thicket,
the Roman silver mine,
crater filled with water
fathoms-deep –

plunge in, break the mirror,
breast the reeds,
strike out toward the golden mean,
breathless, treading water,
limbs not touching – save by chance –
dragon-fly hands darting about the surface,
piston-legs working
down below in the mine.

Sam Riviere

Sam Riviere graduated in Creative and Cultural Studies from Norwich School of Art and Design, where he was taught Creative Writing by George Szirtes and Elspeth Barker. Since then he has published in the *Rialto*, read at the Wells Festival and co-edited a pamphlet of new poets' work. He lives in New Cross, south London.

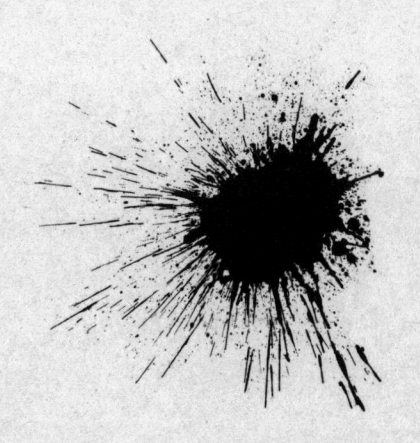

Snap

You had a habit of lying in wait
with a disposable Kodak,
jumping out to catch my face
in a split second of genuine terror.

You collected these shots, pinned up
inside your wardrobe, my eyes
and mouth elastic wide,
hands raised to protect myself.

I never got wise to it,
never failed to blanch, to perform
that slow-motion, startled-cat leap
you found so endlessly amusing.

Now, sifting through prints, I look
for a priceless shot of you to match.
One an unknowing friend took
after I said I wasn't coming back.

I study your face: bleached out,
resenting the shock of the flash.
You couldn't hide it all that well.
Is this unfair? You tell me. Snap.

Sam Riviere

Athens

So here we are, knee-deep in the sewers
of your past, with old gods, spirits,
the bull-headed figures of your ex-boyfriends.
Their faces drift in poorly lit bars
the way drowned faces drift
just below the water's surface.

Here I'm aware of your secrets,
sealed in whitewashed mausoleums,
the gothic apartment block you grew up in;
even the pillars of the acropolis
seem to be hiding something,
picked out on the landscape, clean as bones.

A statue from a classical frieze
guards these sites from me,
with her back to the sun, a missing arm,
the eroded face of an ancient effigy.
I want to hack that look away,
your face, remembered by this city.

The Sex Habits of Insects

Bill's mother, already sloshed, joined us on the veranda
as you amazed us with tales of the sex habits of insects,
how the female mantis devours its mate after coitus,
and will even eat its young.

Bill glowered into the sunset
as it went off like an A-bomb over the bay.
His girlfriend finished with him a year ago; he still wasn't over it.
'Of course, he's terribly depressed,' his mother had warned

in a stage whisper when his back was turned.
Meanwhile I'd committed some inexcusable offence –
you wouldn't look or talk to me directly. Sun glanced
from your shoulder, where you'd slipped your bra straps down

for sunbathing. Bill and I smoked
in silence; you outlined the demise of yet another hapless male,
its spindly limbs fanned from those mechanical jaws, your mouth
and lips stained red by the wine,
when suddenly Bill sat up and screamed 'Look at *me*!'

Sam Riviere

Sprung

Crouched on the stairs in the half-light,
hissing threats to myself, I listened
to the two of you talk half the night.

I could hear almost every word, the tremor
of expectation in your voice,
the assuring rumble of his answers

while I closed and opened my fists,
an insect-crawl on my skin,
the top step gathering mist.

Your little chat was harmless enough,
a hotchpotch of anecdotes
I'd heard before, all familiar stuff.

But that wasn't the point.
It was something much more blunt
that wrestled me into jeans and shirt,

forced me downstairs as if chased,
as if a gun was pressed to my head,
with this look on my face.

Poems

When he met her it was as if he could see
his poems moving around below her skin
like fish in an aquarium. To attract them
he simply tapped the glass of the tank –
and some were pretty big fish. They loomed
close, shadowing her face like a birthmark.
He saw their luminescent scales, the frills
of their fins, their mouths, fat and defenceless,
without natural predators – simply begging
to be caught, mounted and nailed to the wall.

Hotel

It's straight from an art-house film, this scene:
evening light bouncing off the balcony,
the smokers' throat of night traffic starting up.
Back from the beach, you undress and squirm into bed,
warm and brown as bread from the oven.
This is carnality: your skin under a 40-watt bulb,
outside it's dark before we know it. You bow
over my lap devotedly, as if tending a fire.

Hours

There were nights and days, it's fair to say,
when you should have left, but stayed
for those overcast, in-between hours
when I woke to find our heads together,
bodies arranged on the bed
like the frozen hands of a clock.

There was a grey light
which contained the sound of rain
and lent your skin the depthless sheen
of nylon stockings, hazing your hip
where the flesh welled like dammed water.

You said you couldn't sleep
unless I took off my watch. Your heart
contracted, clenched its valves, holding
each beat a fraction too long.

Breakfast

At quarter-past one we spring out of bed like two slices of toast
and tumble downstairs, where sun has buttered the window
and the kitchen swims in Florida orange-juice light.
While I see to coffee she starts the grill, still in her nightie.
From here, I can see the trim crescents of her buttocks
skim the frilled edge of the fabric as she goes up on tiptoes
to reach a high shelf. There, her skin has the matt lustre of
    eggshell.
My stomach growls as she slices the tomatoes into pale pink
    stars.

Text

I could chart your heart's graph with these abbreviated
    messages.
There's evidence enough – how your phone's pacemaker bleep
quickened the pulse, and you felt blood beat in the tip
of your thumb, scrolling down an excess of X's. Your fingers
tapped out code, you read it over, then pressed send,
your winged love-note ricocheting off satellites and towers,
as if you'd rediscovered telepathy, landing
a flashing envelope in his breast pocket, a beating heart.

Sam Riviere

Representation

The painter dreamt the valley long before
he saw it. In recurring dreams he flew
the path of its split lips – a perfect flaw
in God's art. When he woke he drew
its puckered scar. He painted the valley
repeatedly, its scimitar peaks,
deep gulleys and churned creeks,
its rocks ridged like the edge of a key.
He found it by accident, an old man
by then: a swift gash in the land,
an unsealed wound in the tissue
of his brain. Inside its din
of water-echoes, he tasted salt, the fissure
opened, the blue sky rushed in.